ABOUT THE CREATOR

Renée Treml was born and raised in the United States and now lives on the beautiful Surf Coast in Australia. Her stories and illustrations are inspired by nature and influenced by her background in environmental science. When Renée is not writing or illustrating, she can be found walking in the bush or on the beach, or exploring museums, zoos, and aquariums with her family and superenthusiastic little dog.

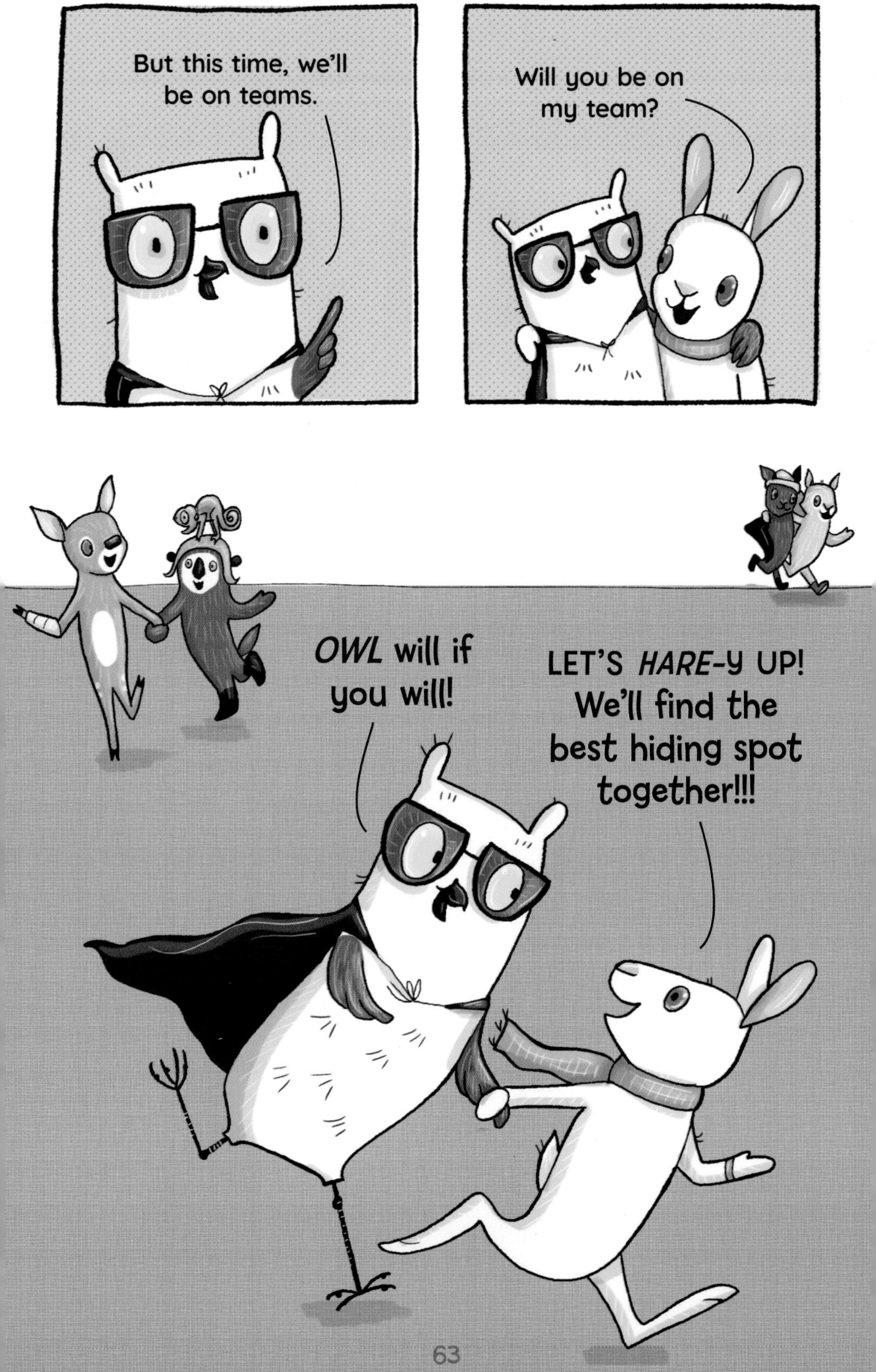
But this time, we'll be on teams.
Will you be on my team?
OWL will if you will!
LET'S *HARE*-y UP! We'll find the best hiding spot together!!!

TABLE OF CONTENTS

CHAPTER 1

HIDE AND *SQUEAK*

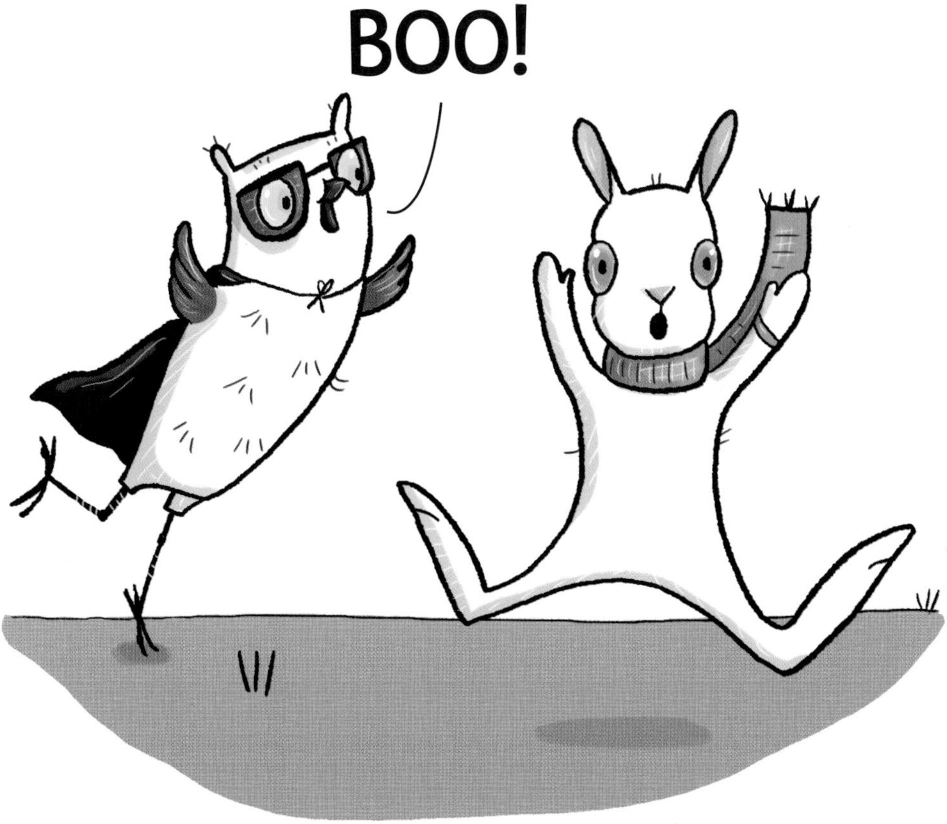
BOO!

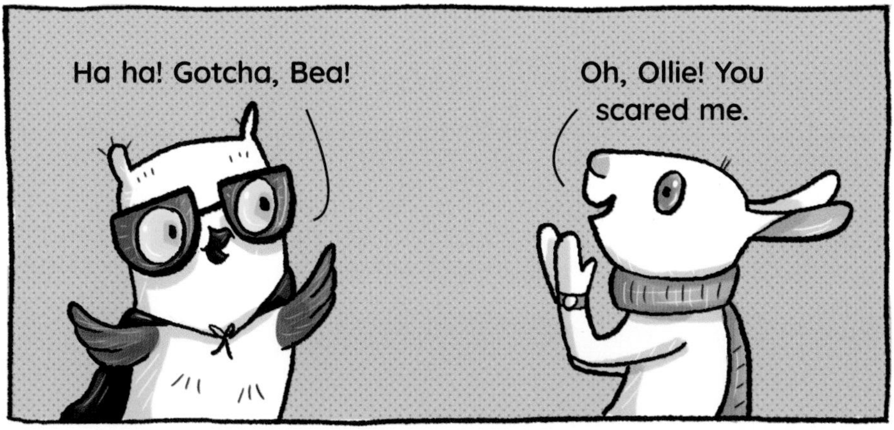
Ha ha! Gotcha, Bea!
Oh, Ollie! You scared me.

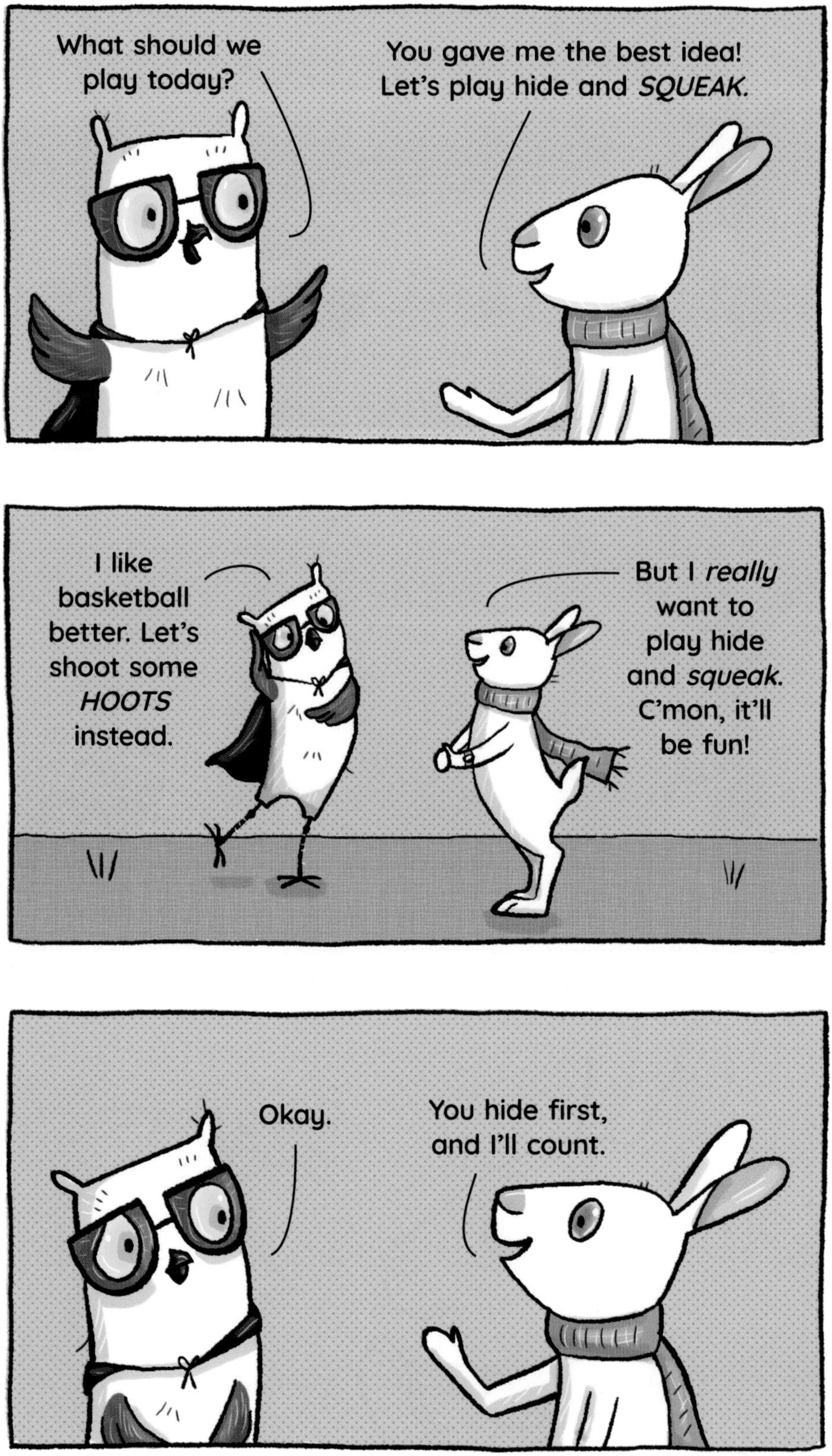
What should we play today?
You gave me the best idea! Let's play hide and *SQUEAK.*
I like basketball better. Let's shoot some *HOOTS* instead.
But I *really* want to play hide and *squeak.* C'mon, it'll be fun!
Okay.
You hide first, and I'll count.

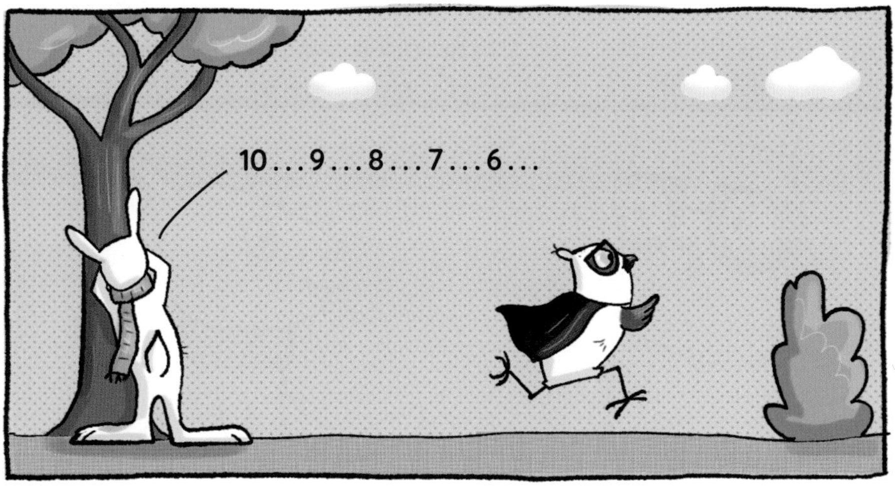
10...9...8...7...6...

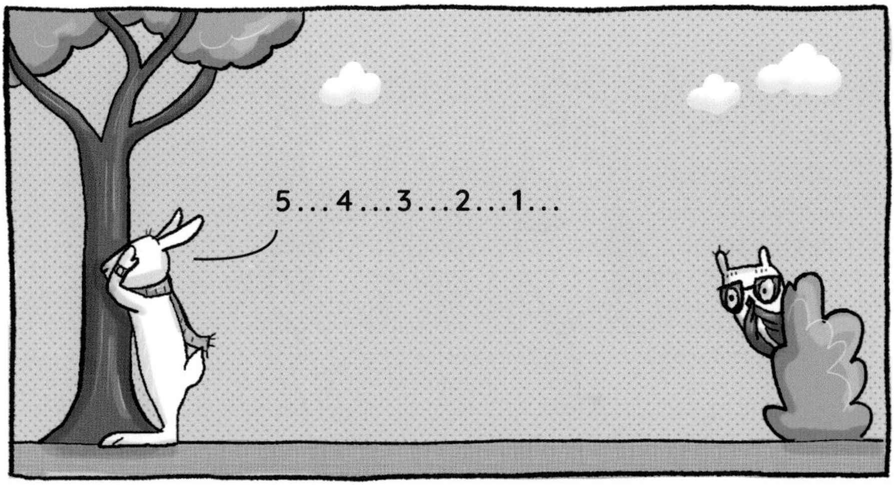
5...4...3...2...1...

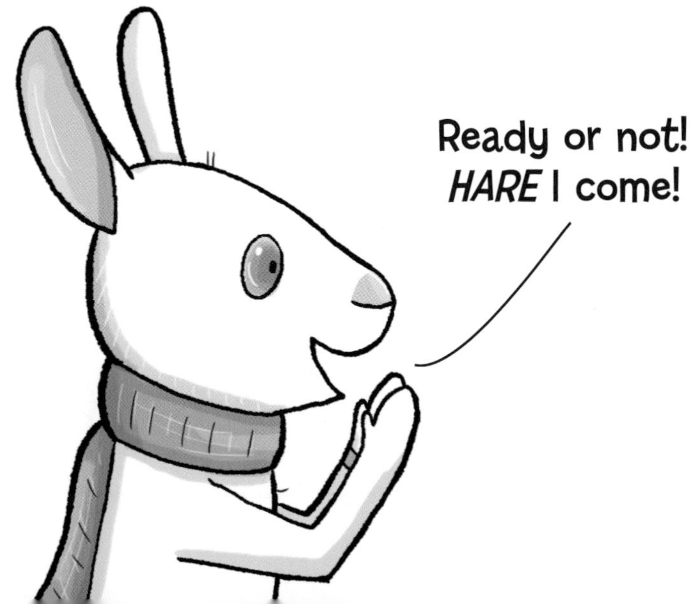
Ready or not!
HARE I come!

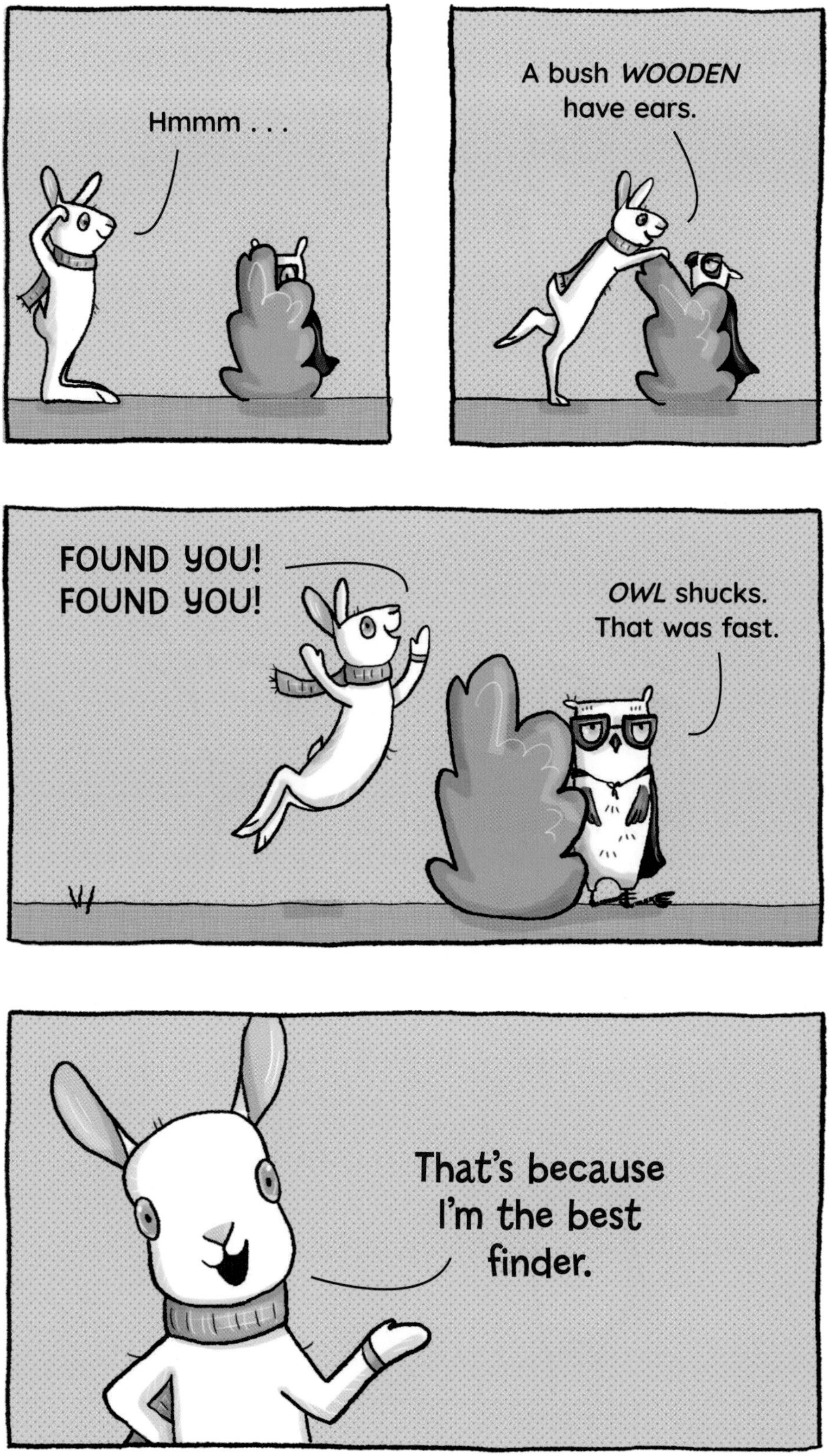
Hmmm . . .
A bush *WOODEN* have ears.
FOUND YOU! FOUND YOU!
OWL shucks. That was fast.
That's because I'm the best finder.

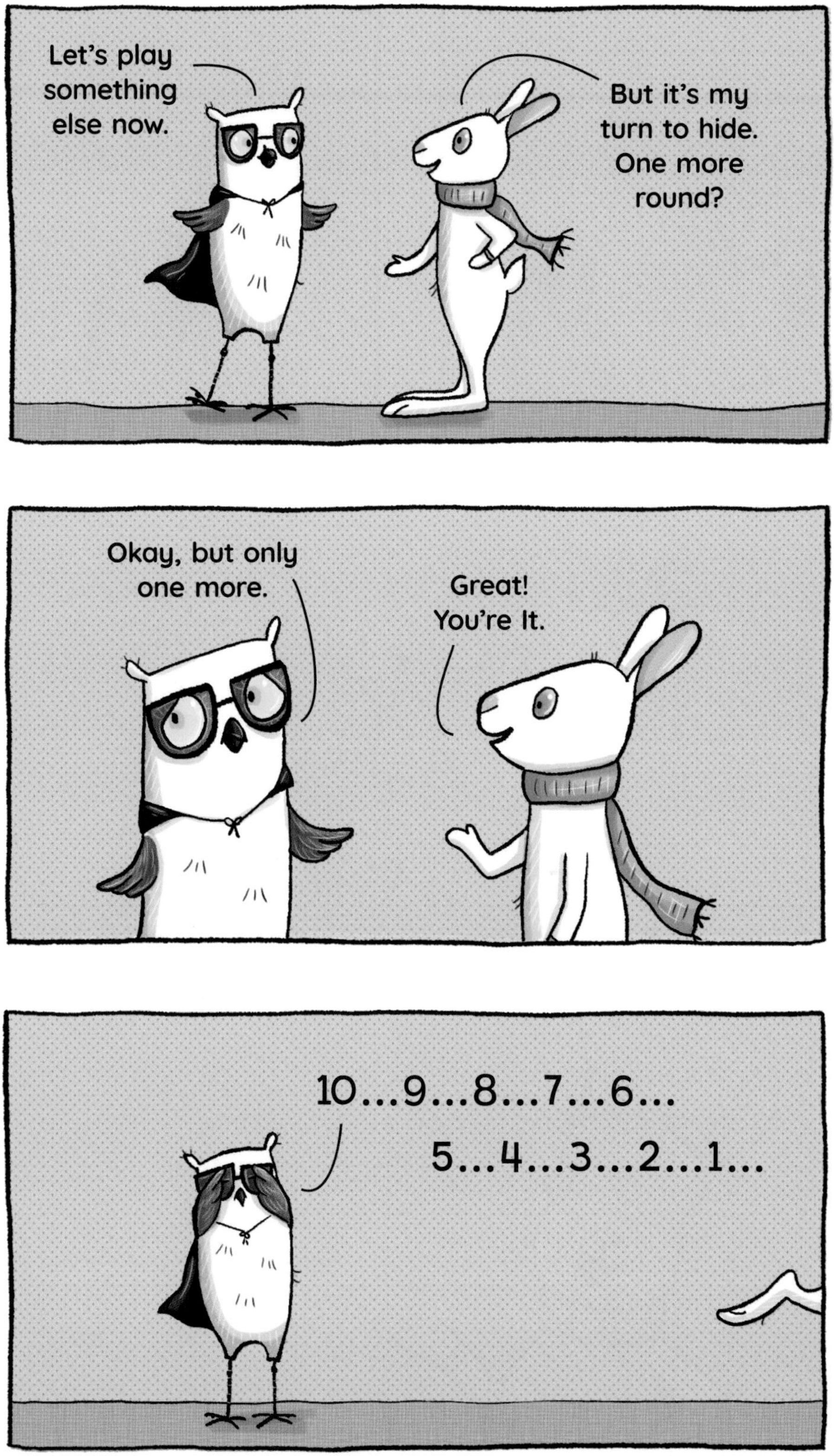
Let's play something else now.
But it's my turn to hide. One more round?
Okay, but only one more.
Great! You're It.
10...9...8...7...6...
5...4...3...2...1...

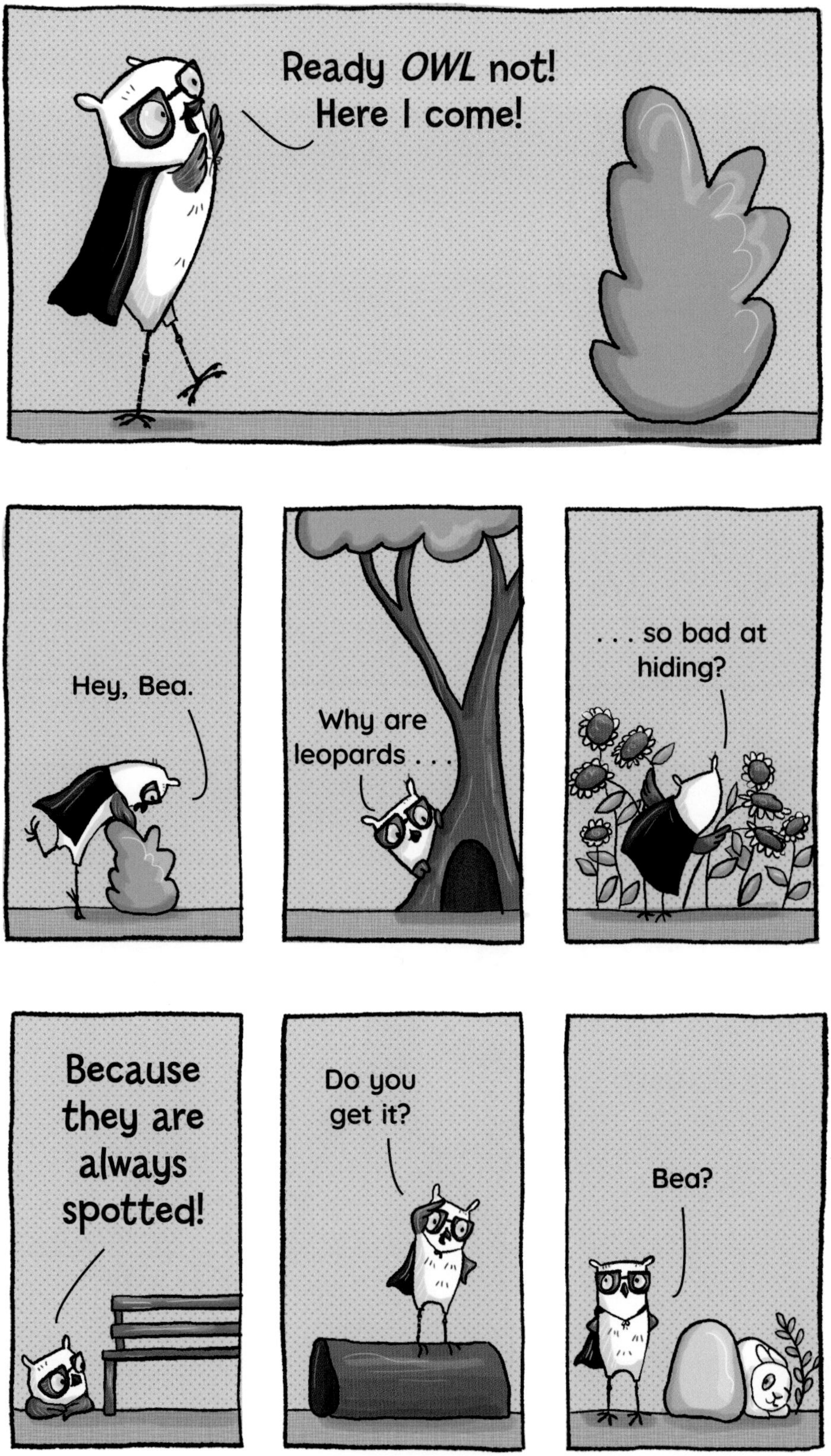

Ready *OWL* not!
Here I come!
Hey, Bea.
Why are leopards . . .
. . . so bad at hiding?
Because they are always spotted!
Do you get it?
Bea?

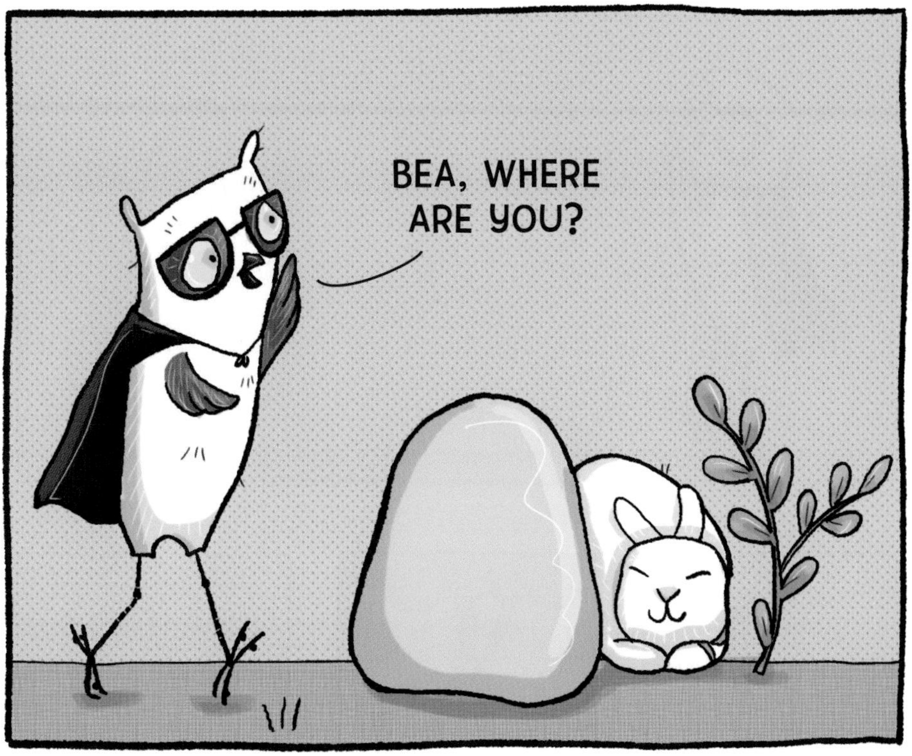
BEA, WHERE ARE YOU?

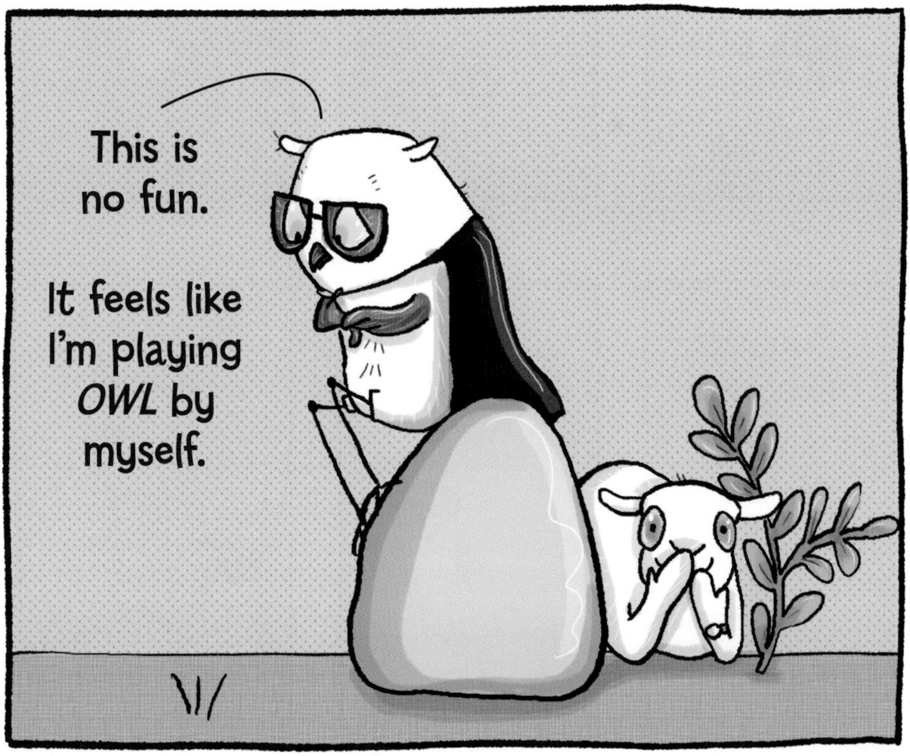
This is no fun.
It feels like I'm playing *OWL* by myself.

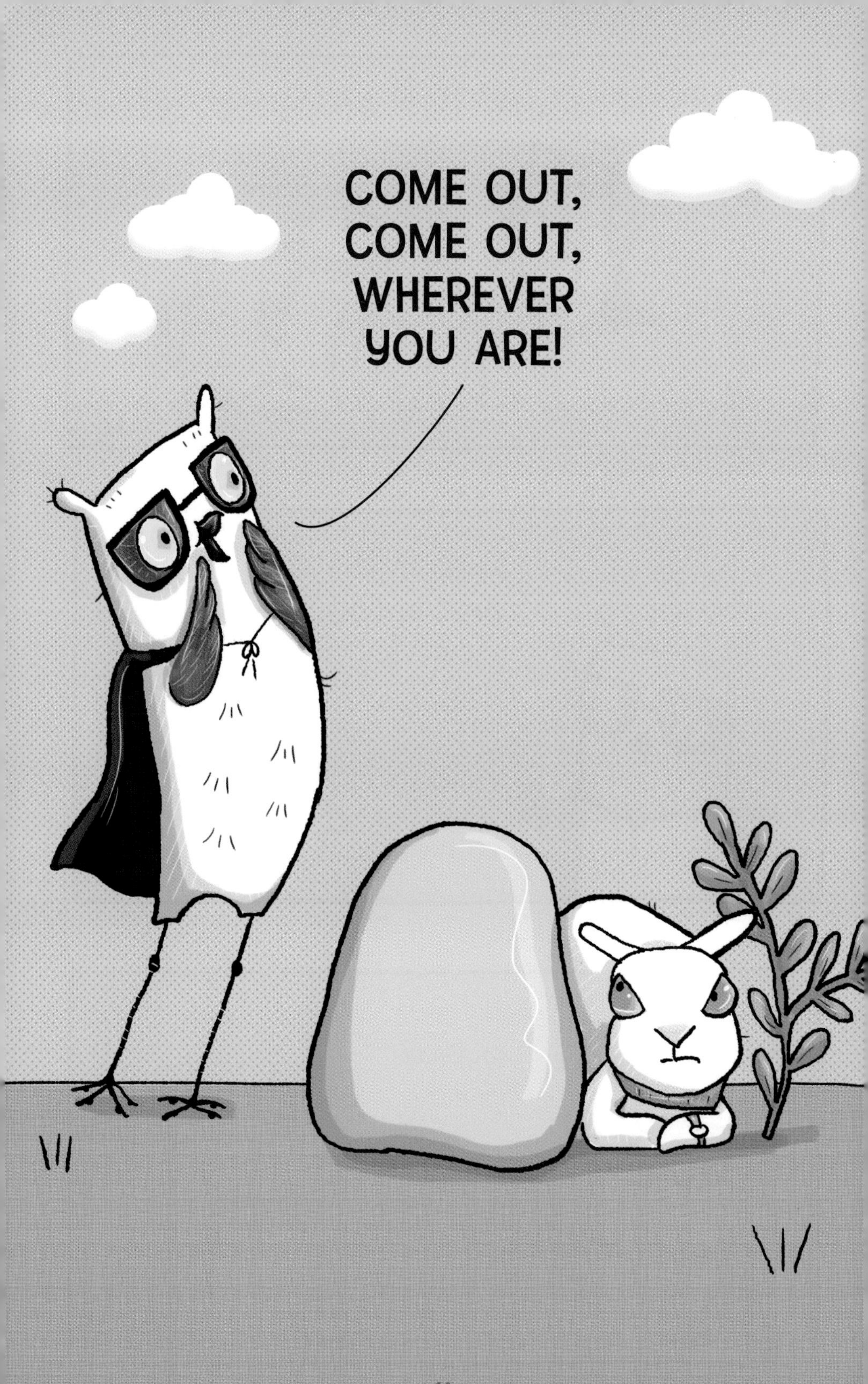
COME OUT, COME OUT, WHEREVER YOU ARE!

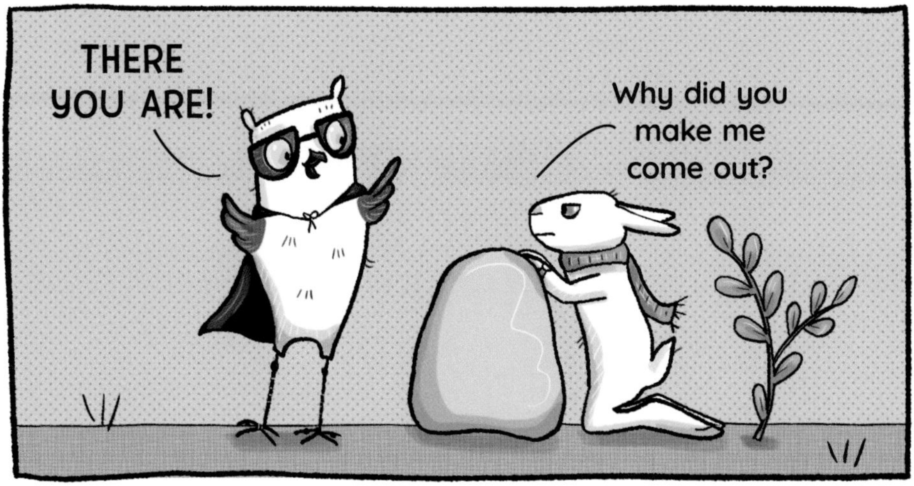
THERE YOU ARE!
Why did you make me come out?
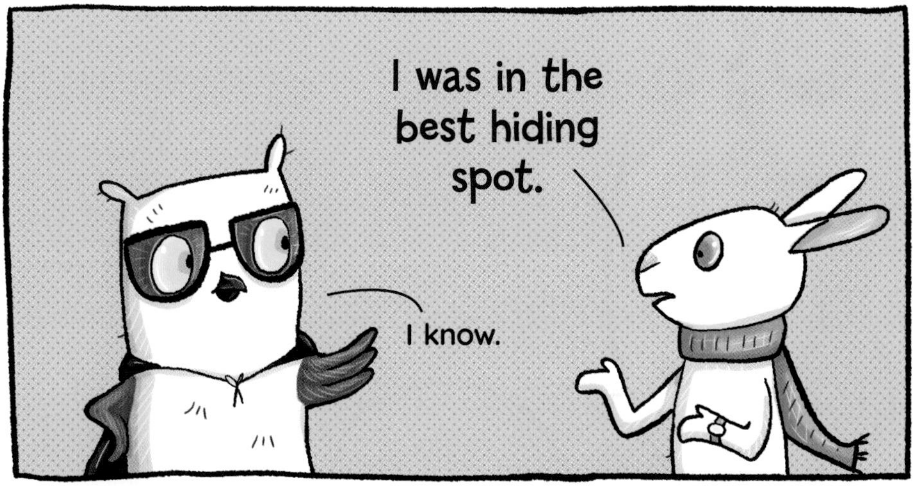
I was in the best hiding spot.
I know.
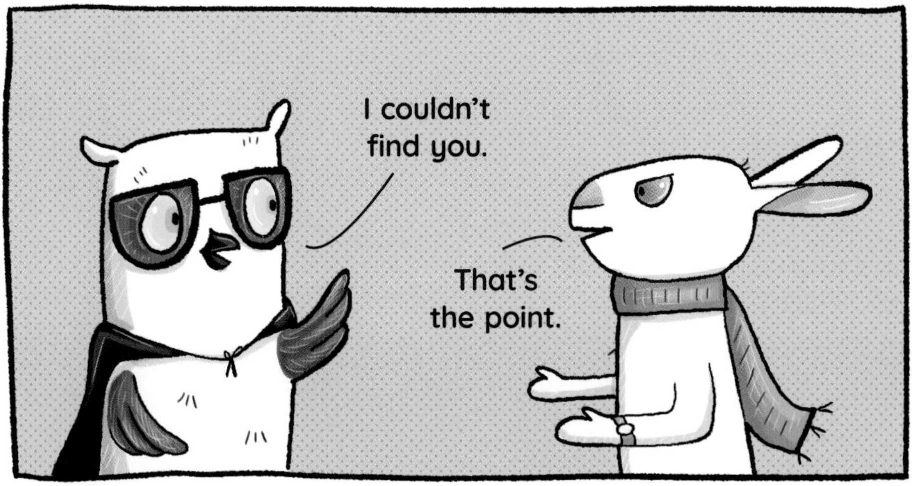
I couldn't find you.
That's the point.

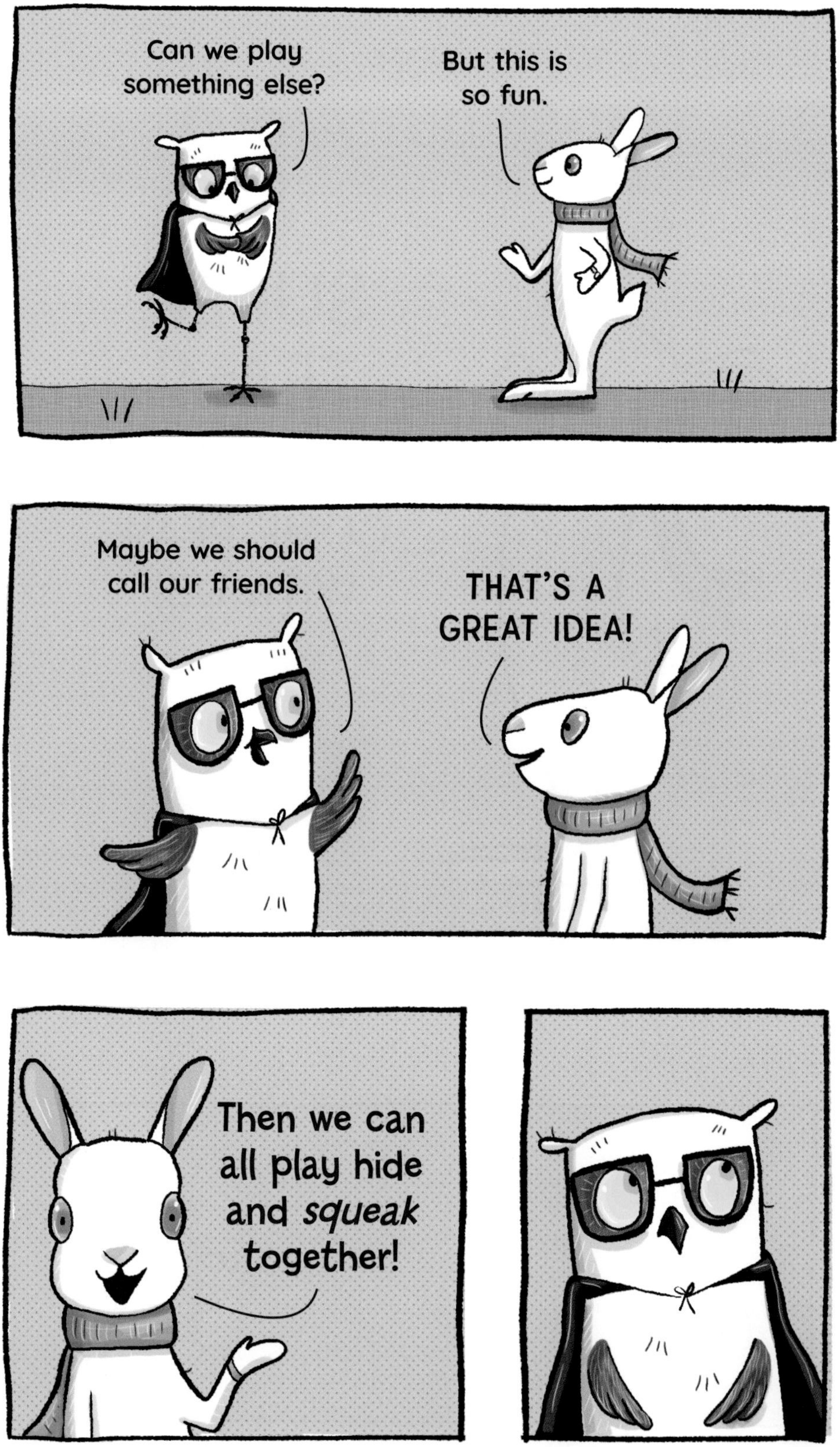
Can we play something else?
But this is so fun.
Maybe we should call our friends.
THAT'S A GREAT IDEA!
Then we can all play hide and *squeak* together!

CHAPTER 2

LAUGH OUT *PROUD*

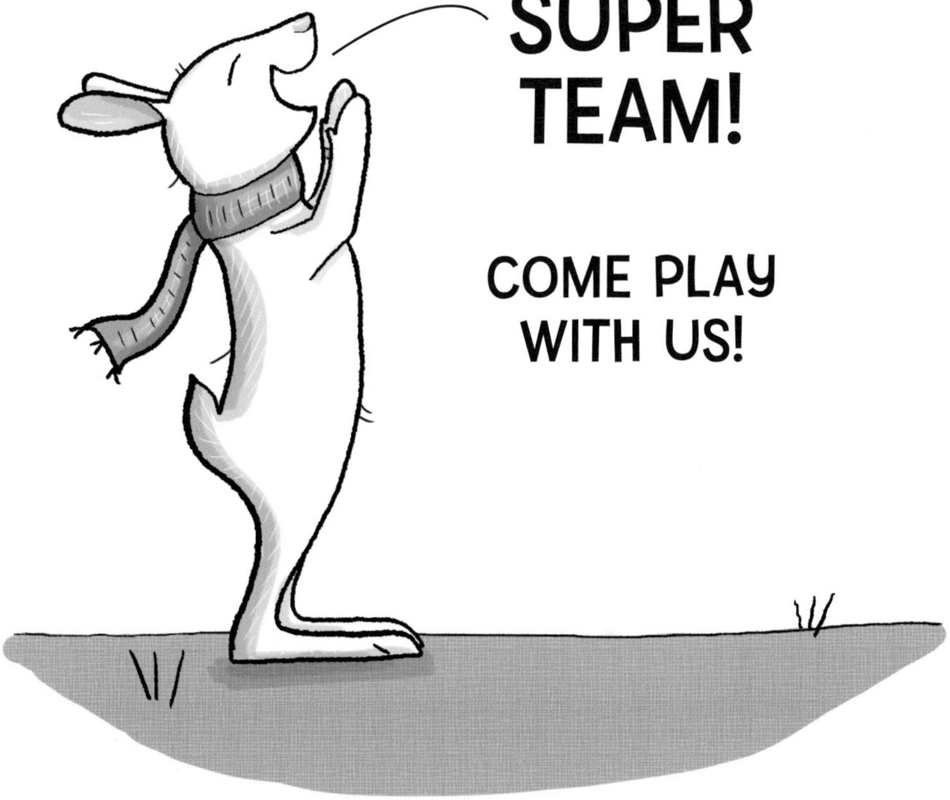
SUPER TEAM!
COME PLAY WITH US!

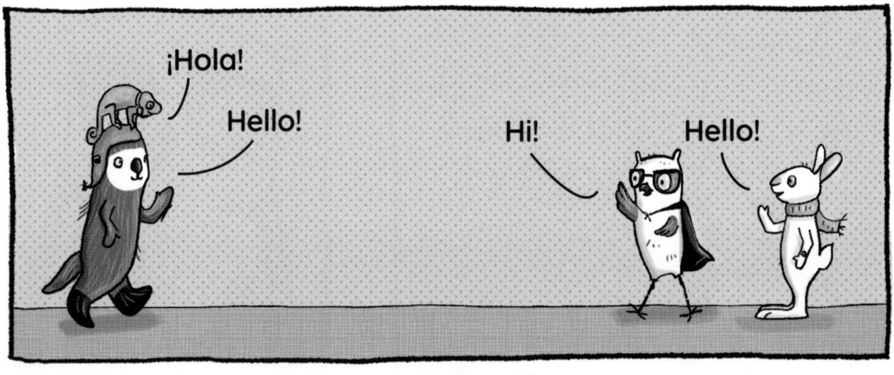
¡Hola!
Hello!
Hi!
Hello!

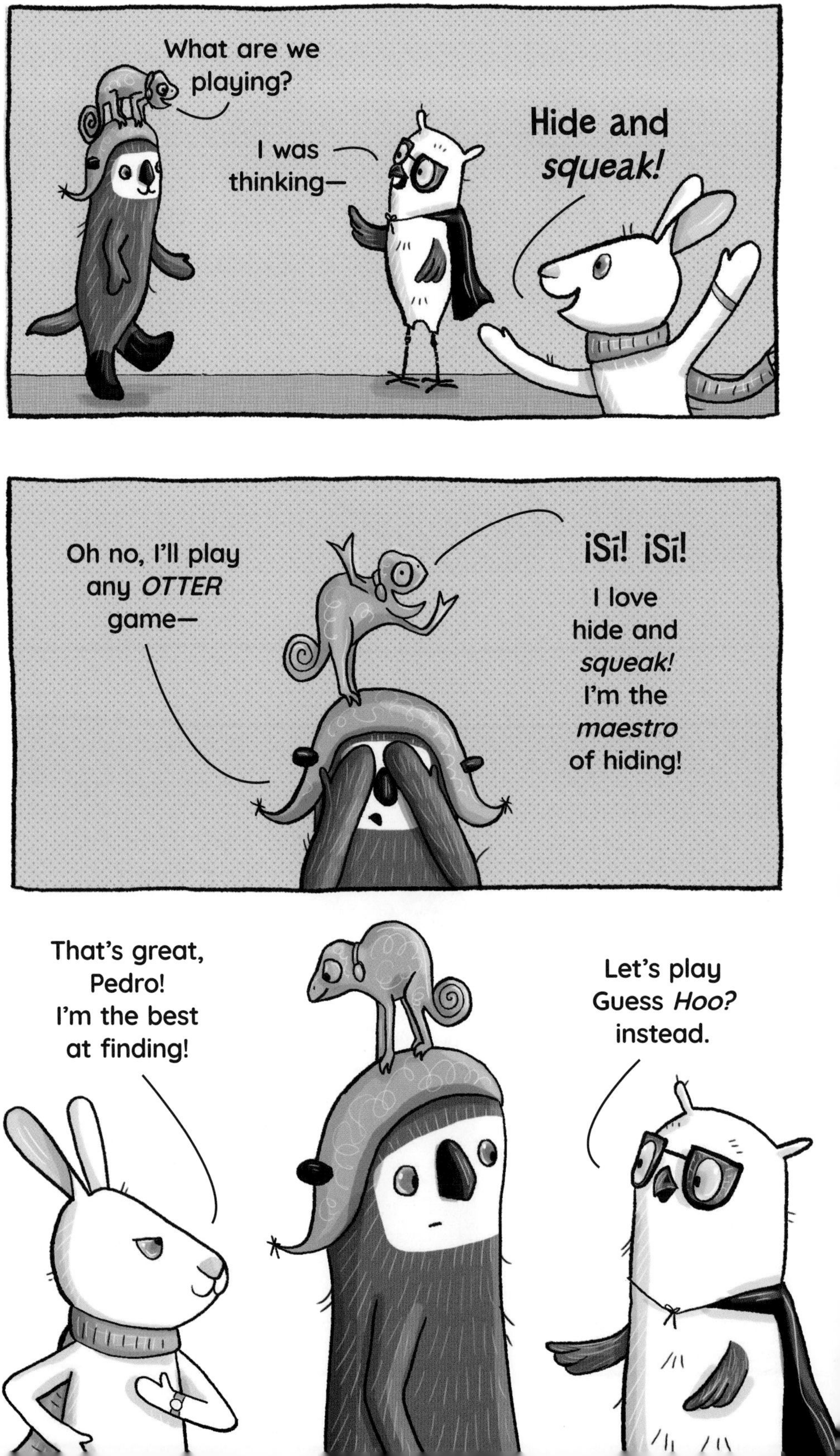
What are we playing?
I was thinking—
Hide and *squeak!*
Oh no, I'll play any *OTTER* game—
¡Sí! ¡Sí!
I love hide and *squeak!* I'm the *maestro* of hiding!
That's great, Pedro! I'm the best at finding!
Let's play Guess *Hoo?* instead.

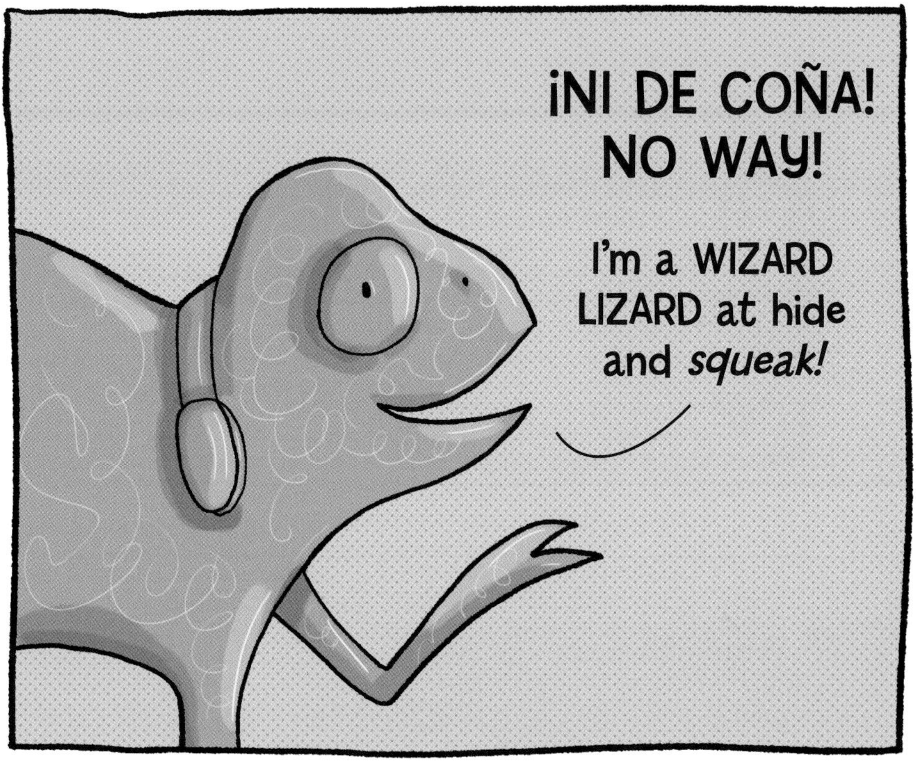
¡NI DE COÑA!
NO WAY!
I'm a WIZARD LIZARD at hide and *squeak!*

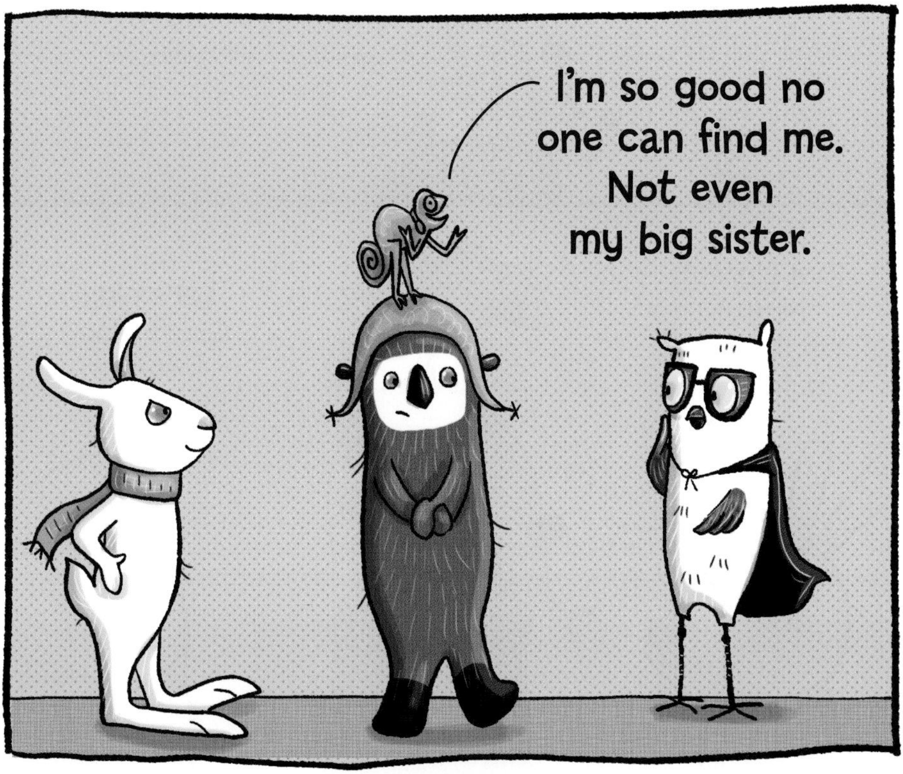
I'm so good no one can find me. Not even my big sister.

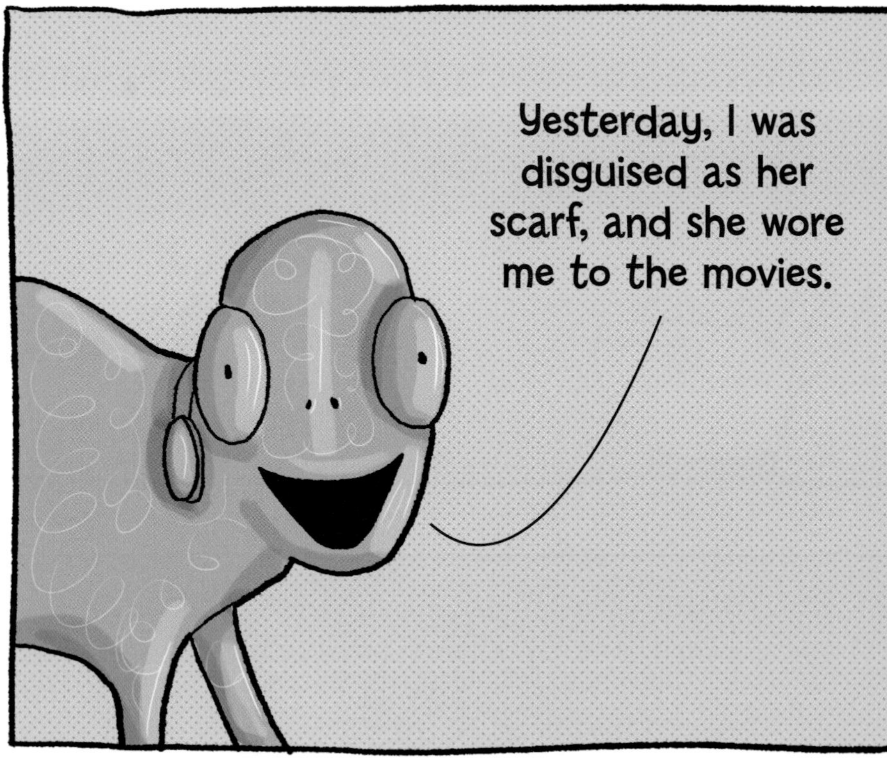
Yesterday, I was disguised as her scarf, and she wore me to the movies.

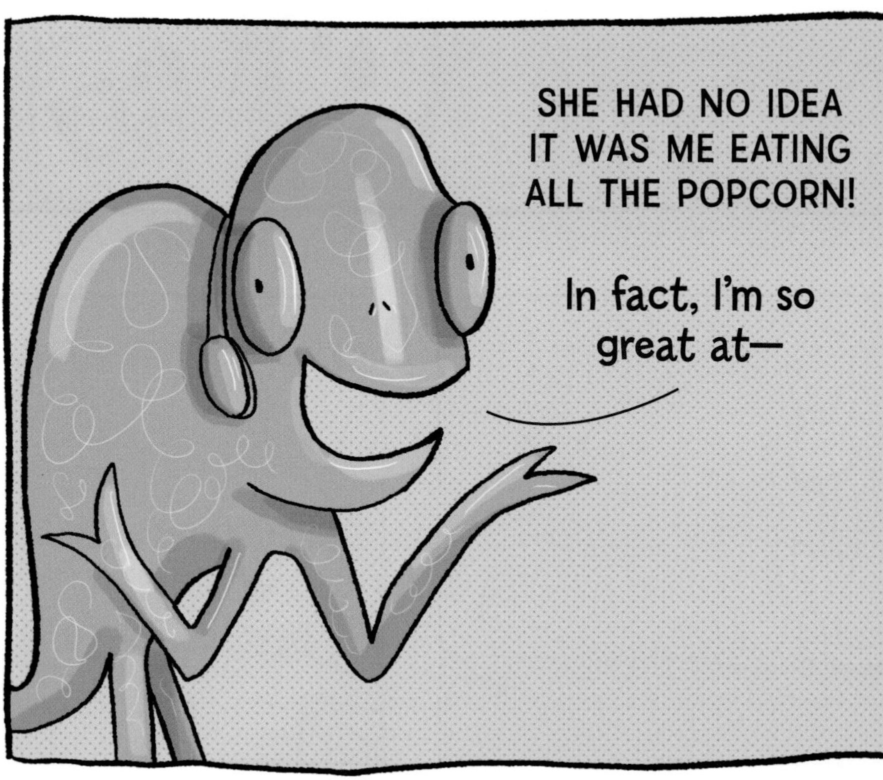
SHE HAD NO IDEA IT WAS ME EATING ALL THE POPCORN!
In fact, I'm so great at—

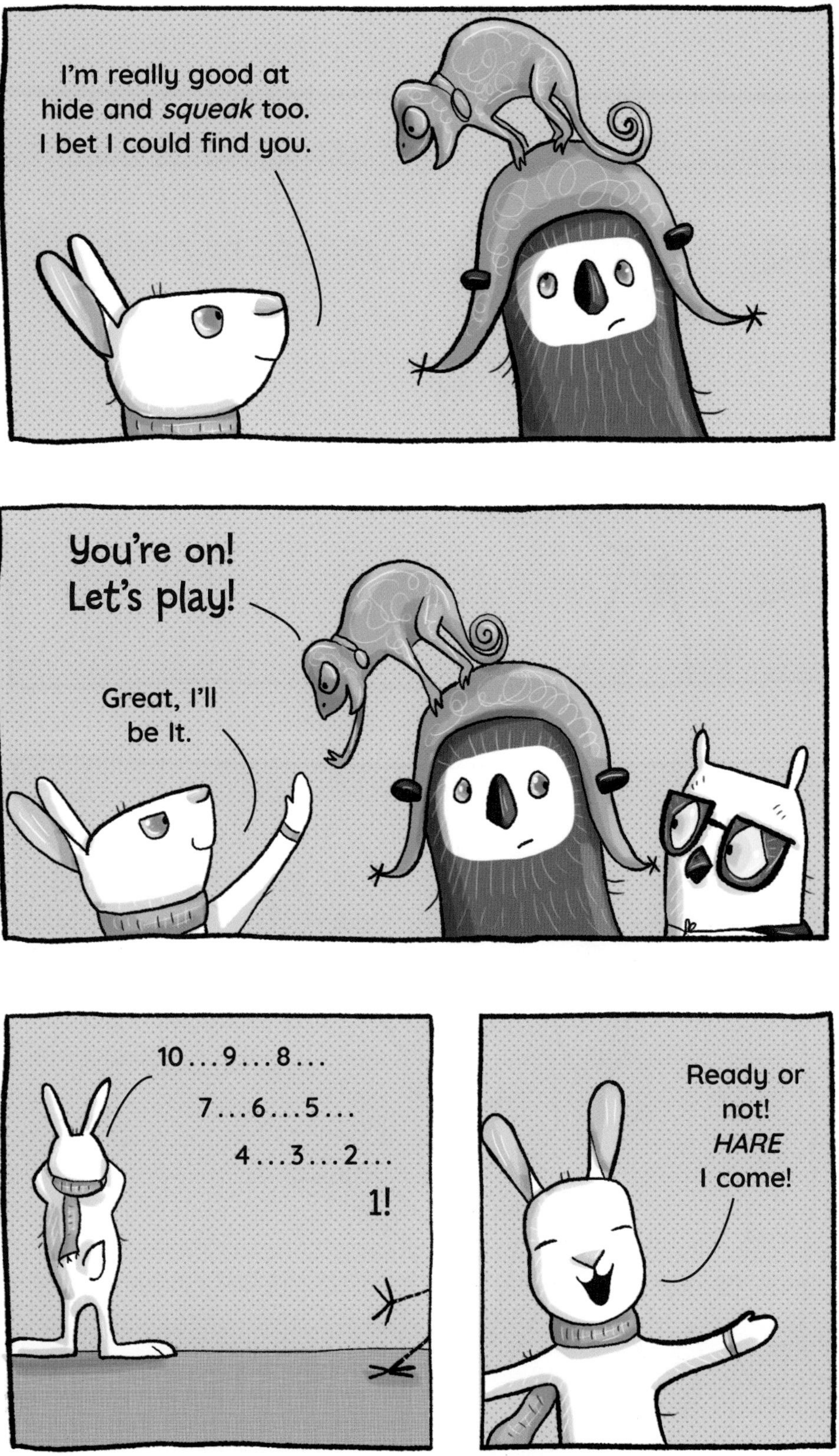
I'm really good at hide and *squeak* too. I bet I could find you.
You're on! Let's play!
Great, I'll be It.
10...9...8...
7...6...5...
4...3...2...
1!
Ready or not! *HARE* I come!

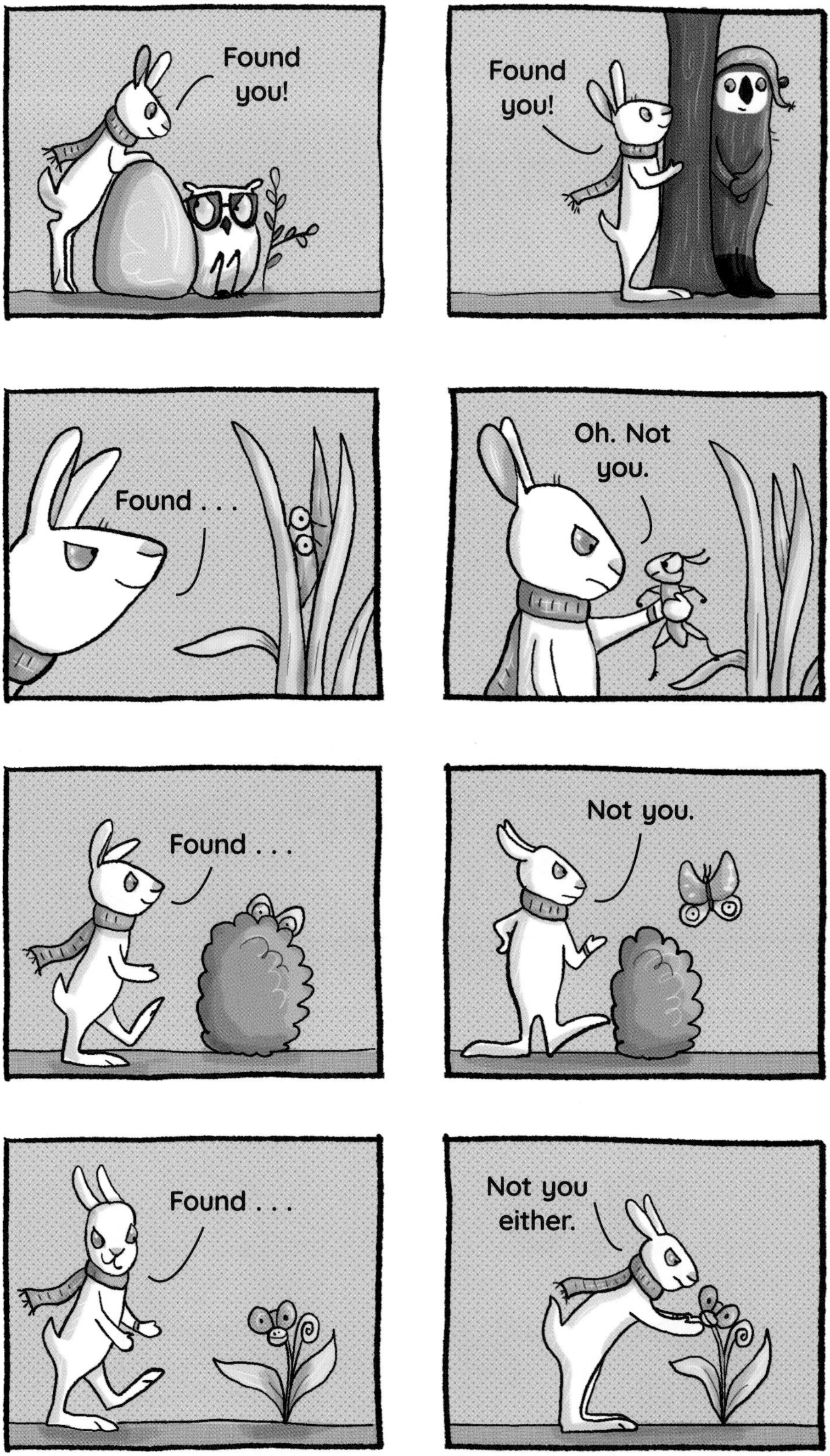
Found you!
Found you!
Found . . .
Oh. Not you.
Found . . .
Not you.
Found . . .
Not you either.

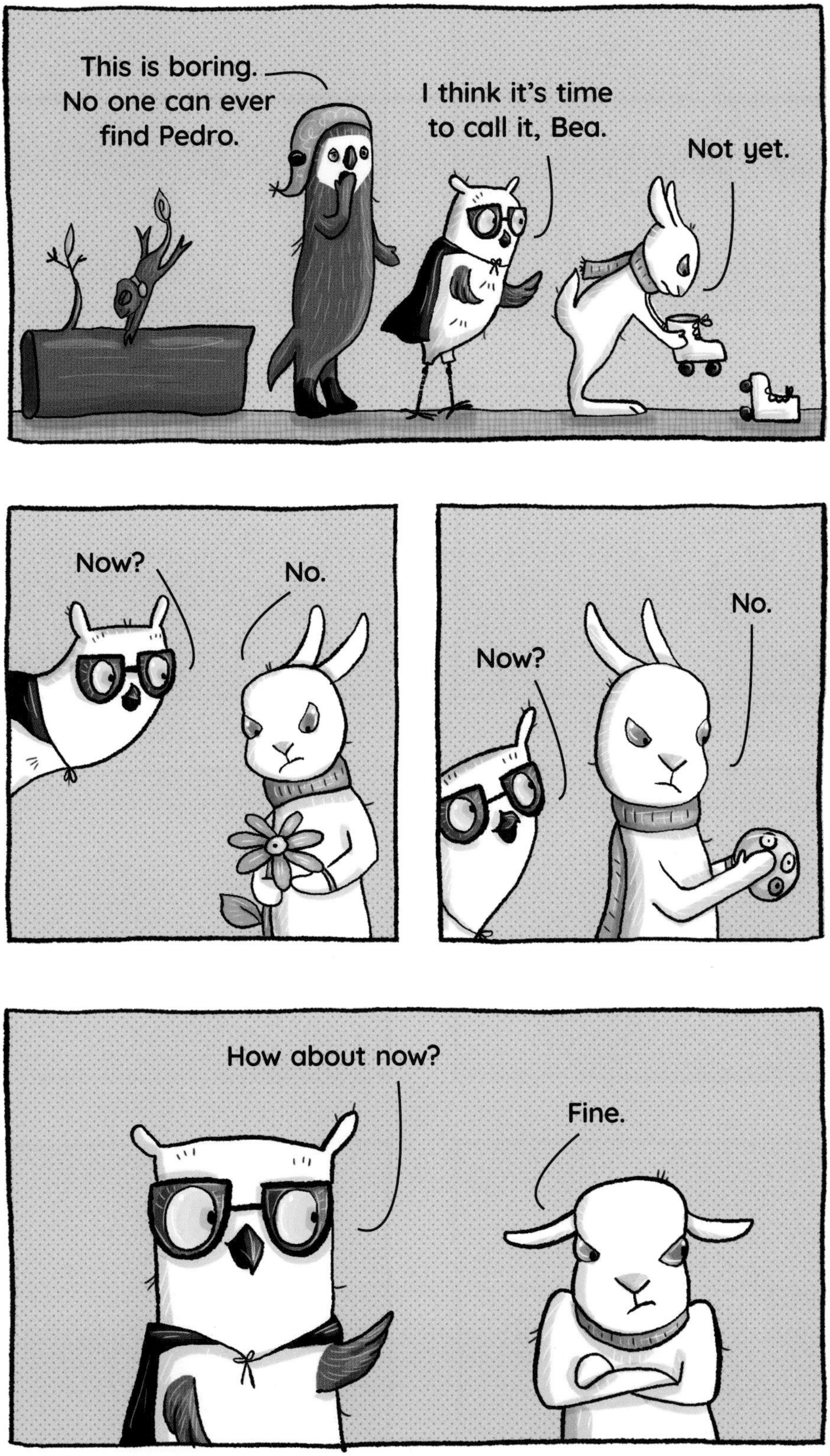

This is boring. No one can ever find Pedro.
I think it's time to call it, Bea.
Not yet.
Now?
No.
Now?
No.
How about now?
Fine.

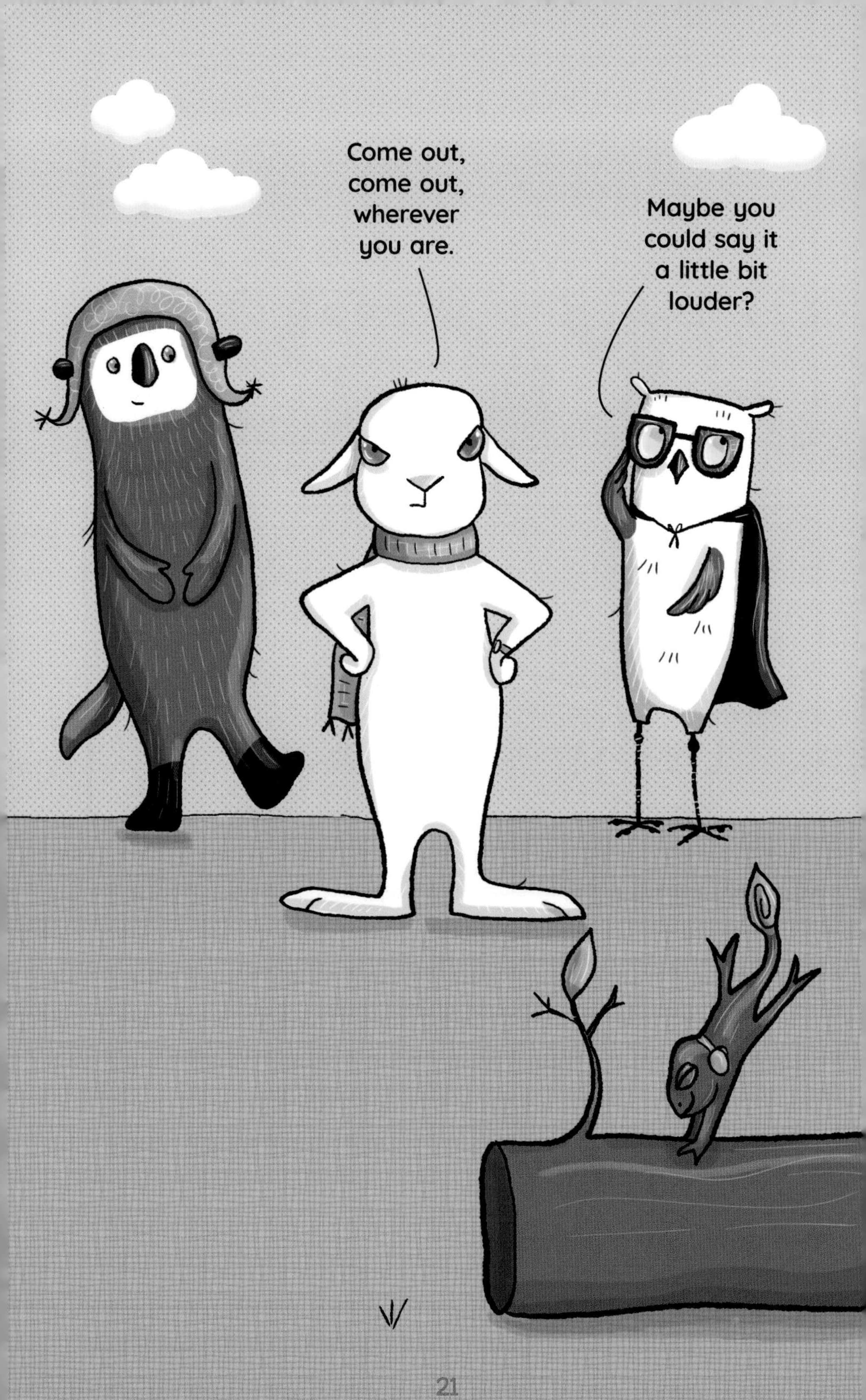
Come out, come out, wherever you are.
Maybe you could say it a little bit louder?

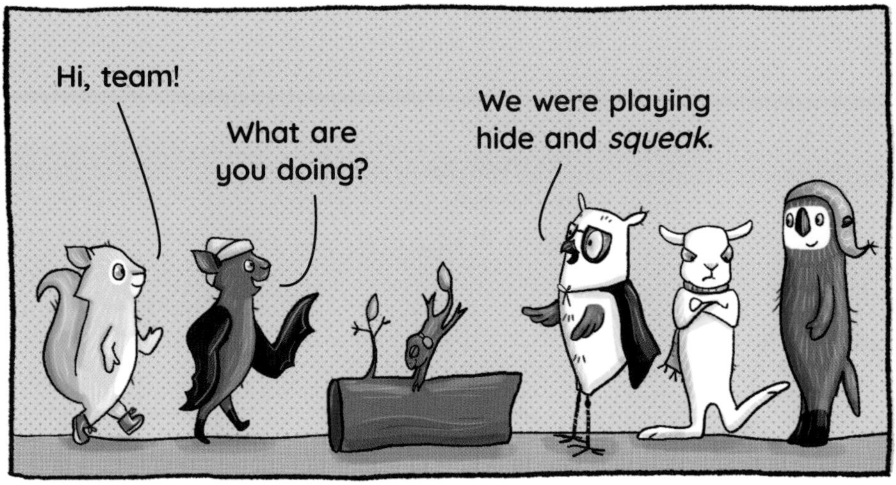
Hi, team!
What are you doing?
We were playing hide and *squeak*.

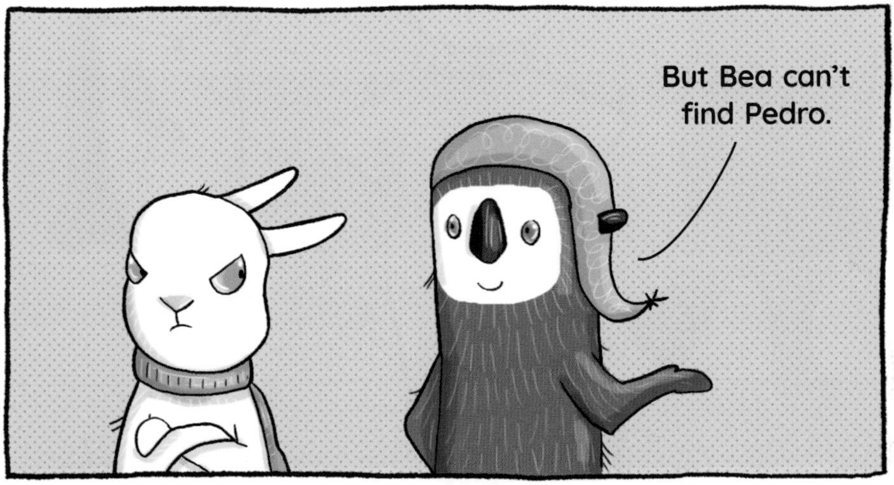
But Bea can't find Pedro.

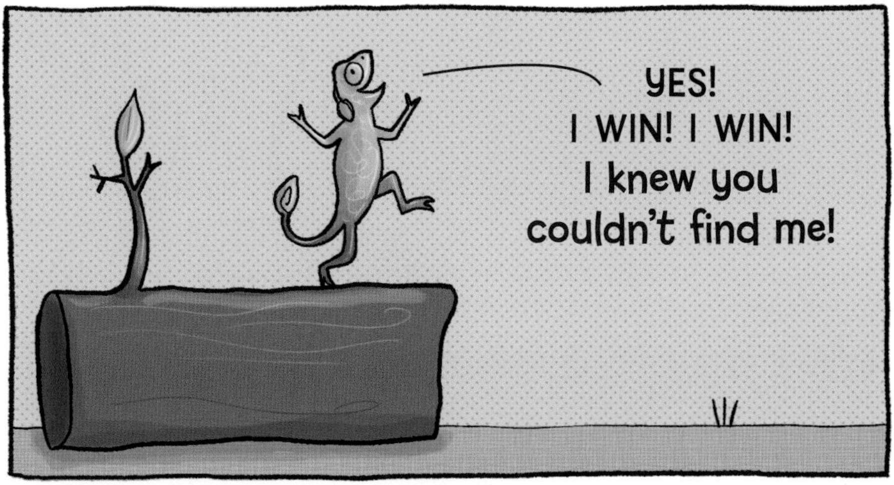
YES!
I WIN! I WIN!
I knew you couldn't find me!

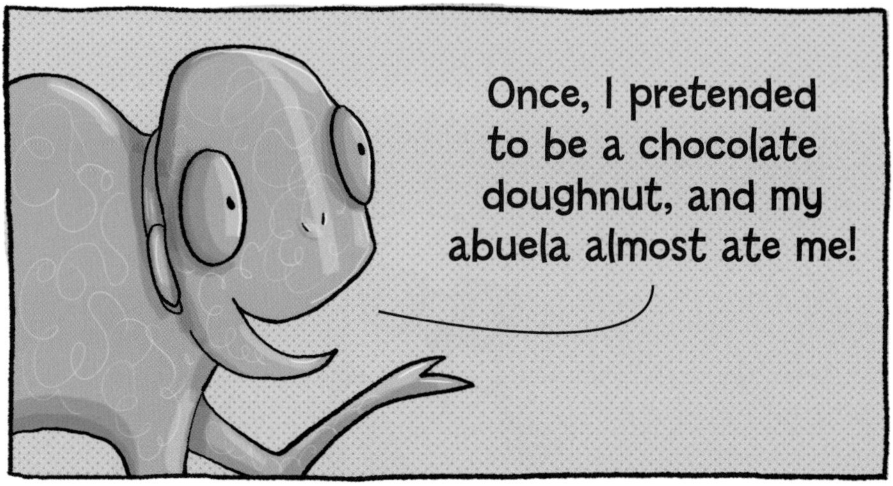
Once, I pretended to be a chocolate doughnut, and my abuela almost ate me!

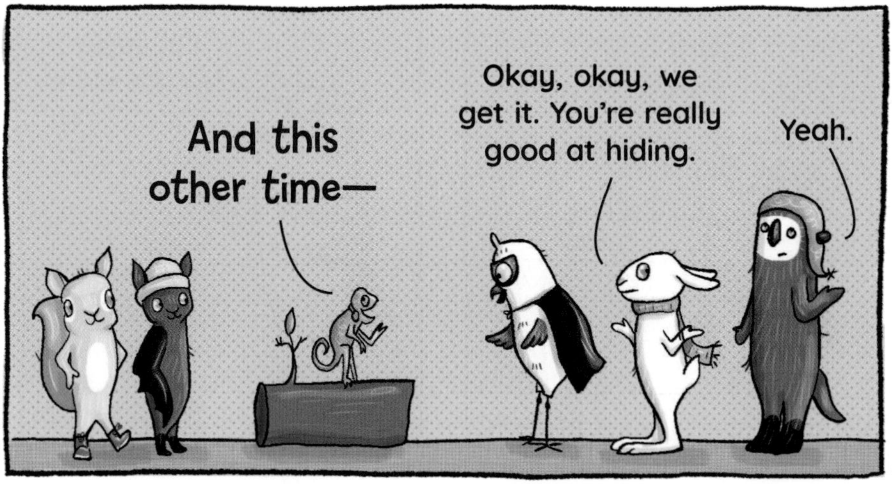
And this other time—
Okay, okay, we get it. You're really good at hiding.
Yeah.

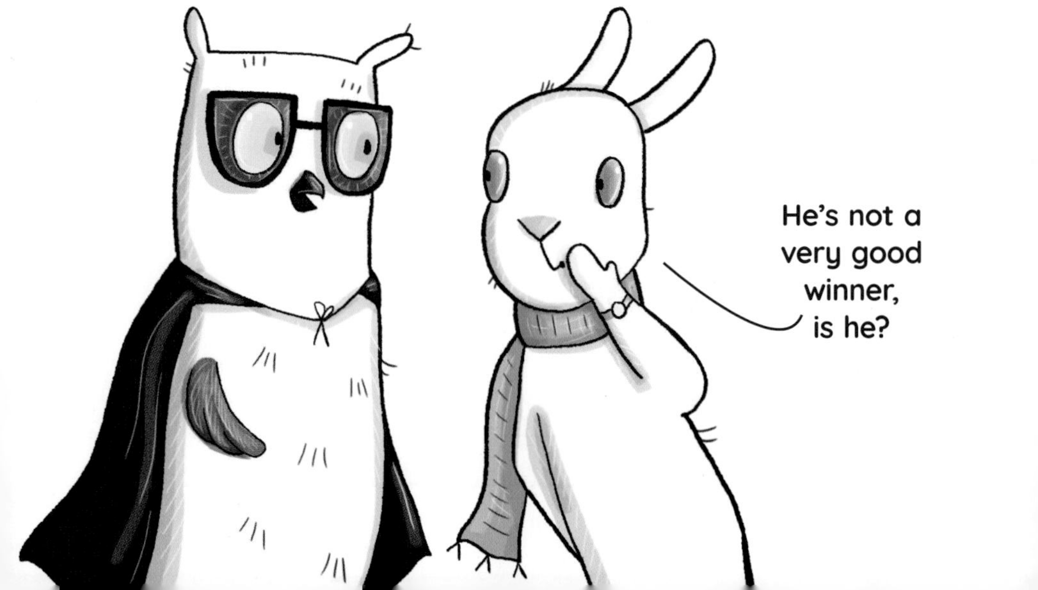
He's not a very good winner, is he?

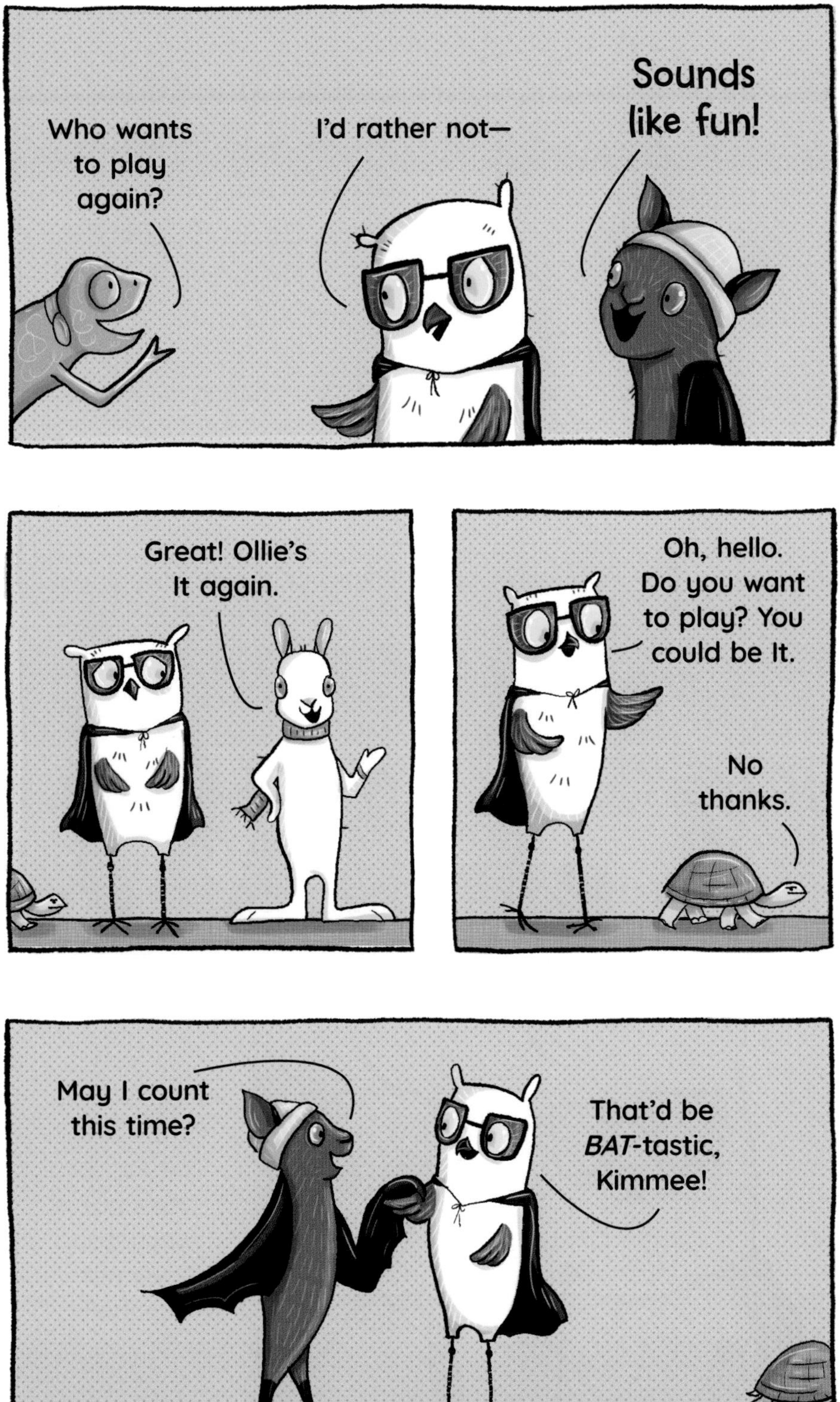
Who wants to play again?
I'd rather not—
Sounds like fun!
Great! Ollie's It again.
Oh, hello. Do you want to play? You could be It.
No thanks.
May I count this time?
That'd be *BAT*-tastic, Kimmee!

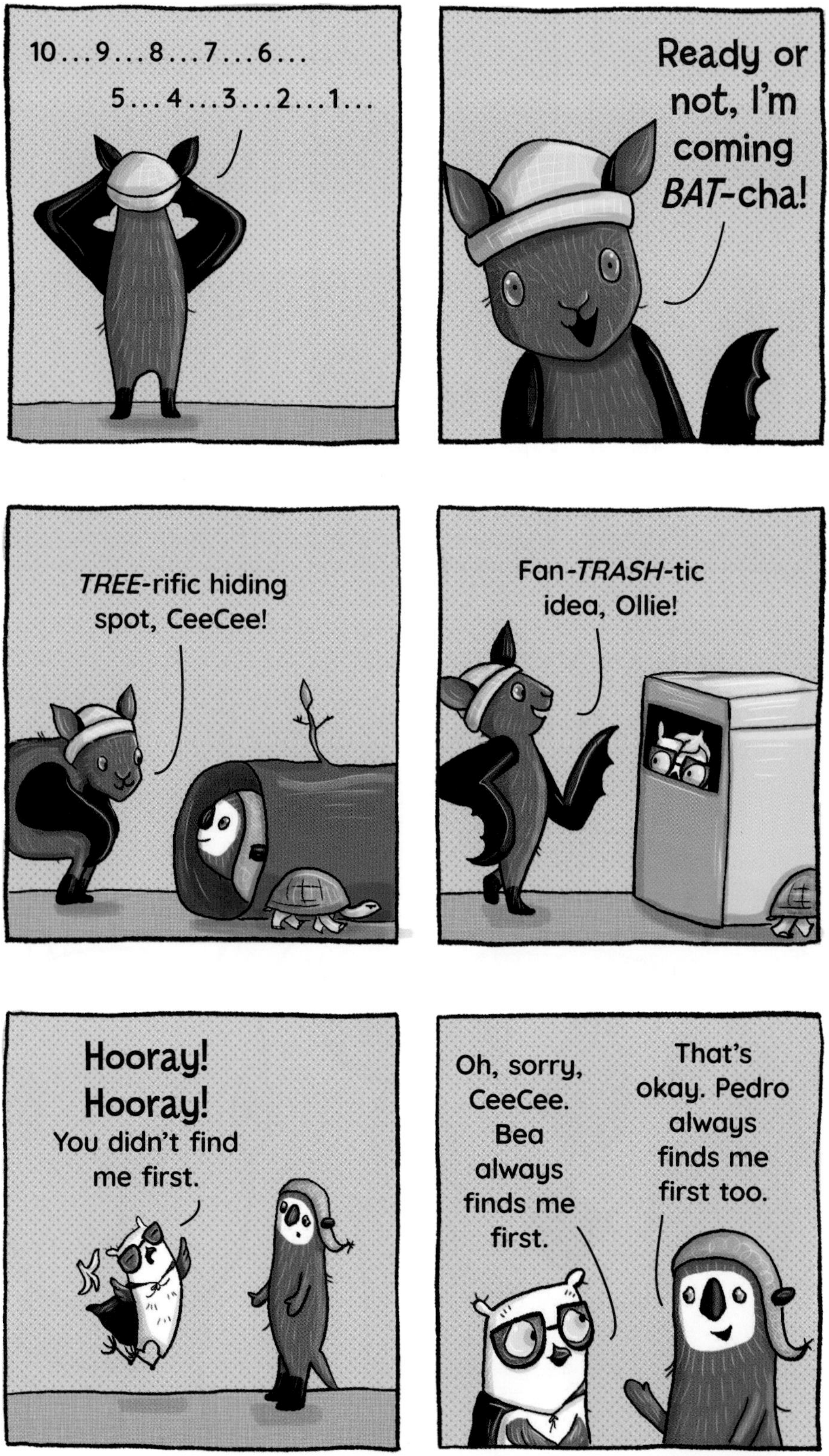
10...9...8...7...6...
5...4...3...2...1...
Ready or not, I'm coming *BAT*-cha!
TREE-rific hiding spot, CeeCee!
Fan-*TRASH*-tic idea, Ollie!
Hooray! Hooray! You didn't find me first.
Oh, sorry, CeeCee. Bea always finds me first.
That's okay. Pedro always finds me first too.

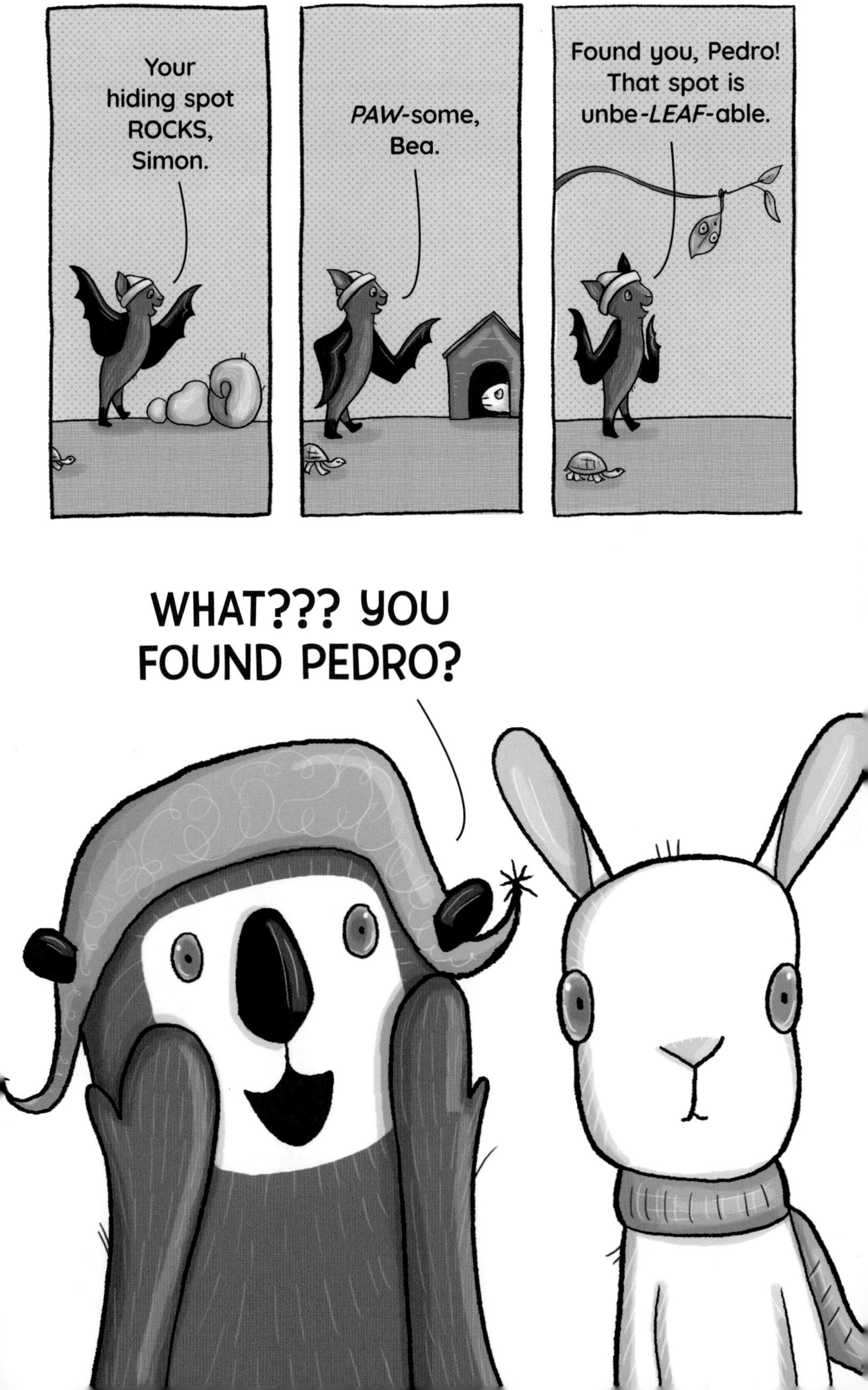
Your hiding spot ROCKS, Simon.
PAW-some, Bea.
Found you, Pedro! That spot is unbe-LEAF-able.
WHAT??? YOU FOUND PEDRO?

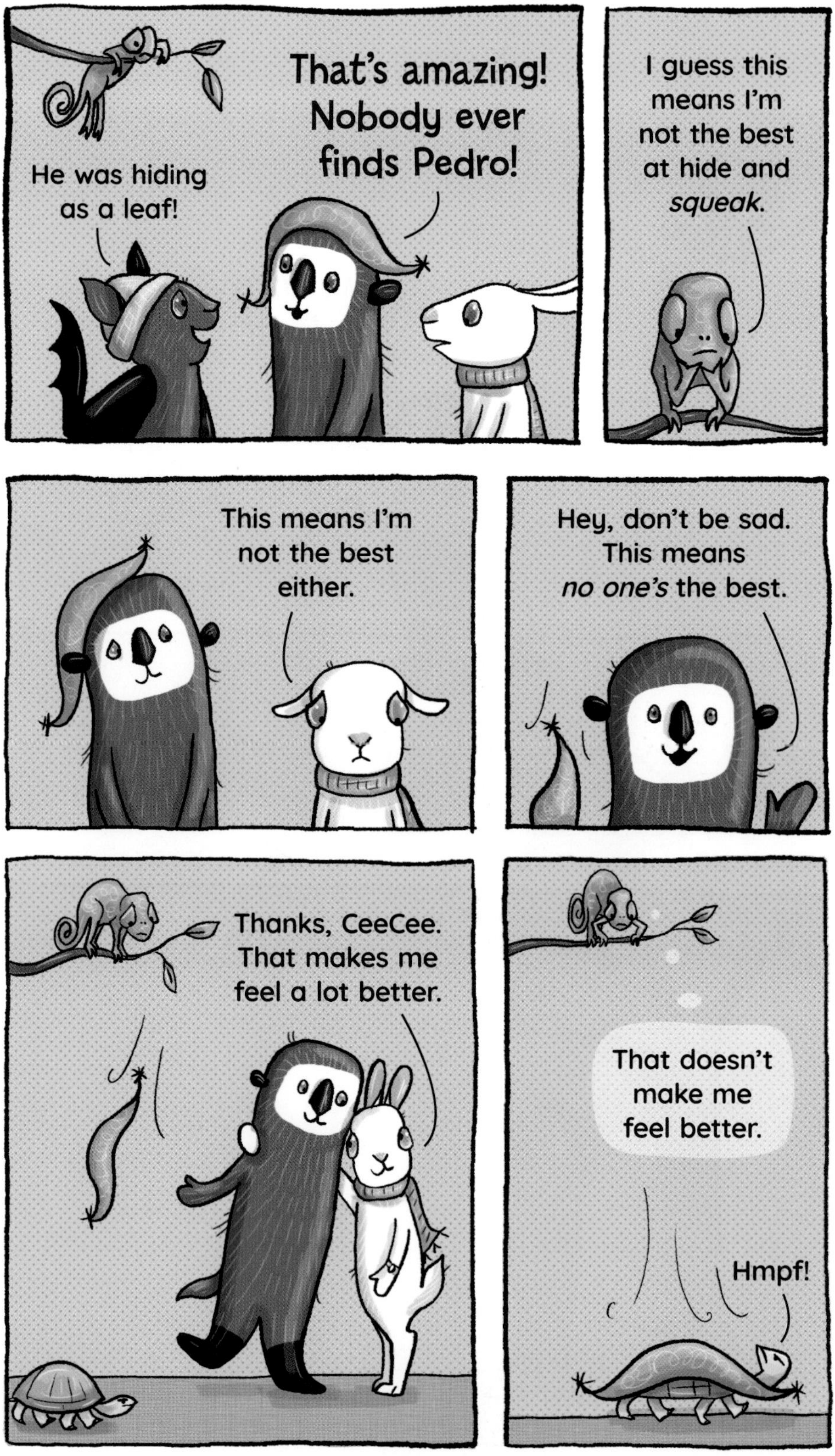

That's amazing! Nobody ever finds Pedro!
He was hiding as a leaf!
I guess this means I'm not the best at hide and *squeak*.
This means I'm not the best either.
Hey, don't be sad. This means *no one's* the best.
Thanks, CeeCee. That makes me feel a lot better.
That doesn't make me feel better.
Hmpf!

CHAPTER 3
BAT TRICK

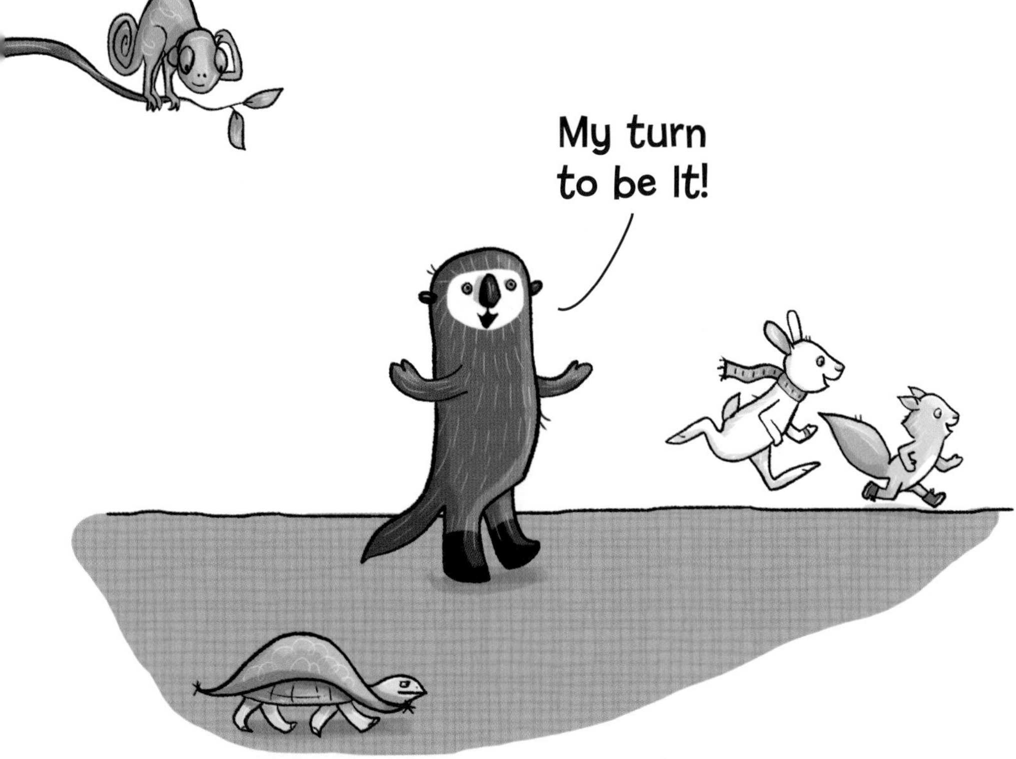
My turn to be It!

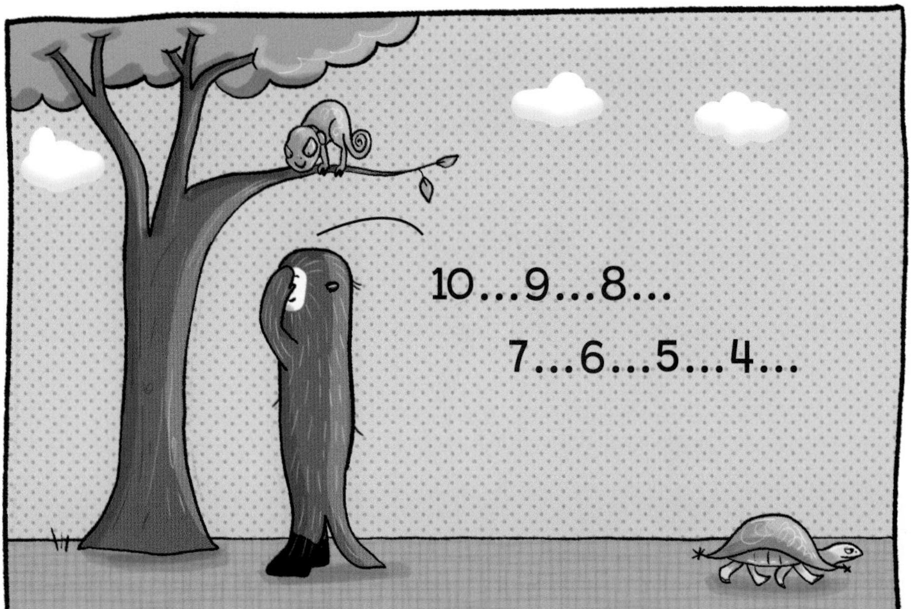
10...9...8...
7...6...5...4...

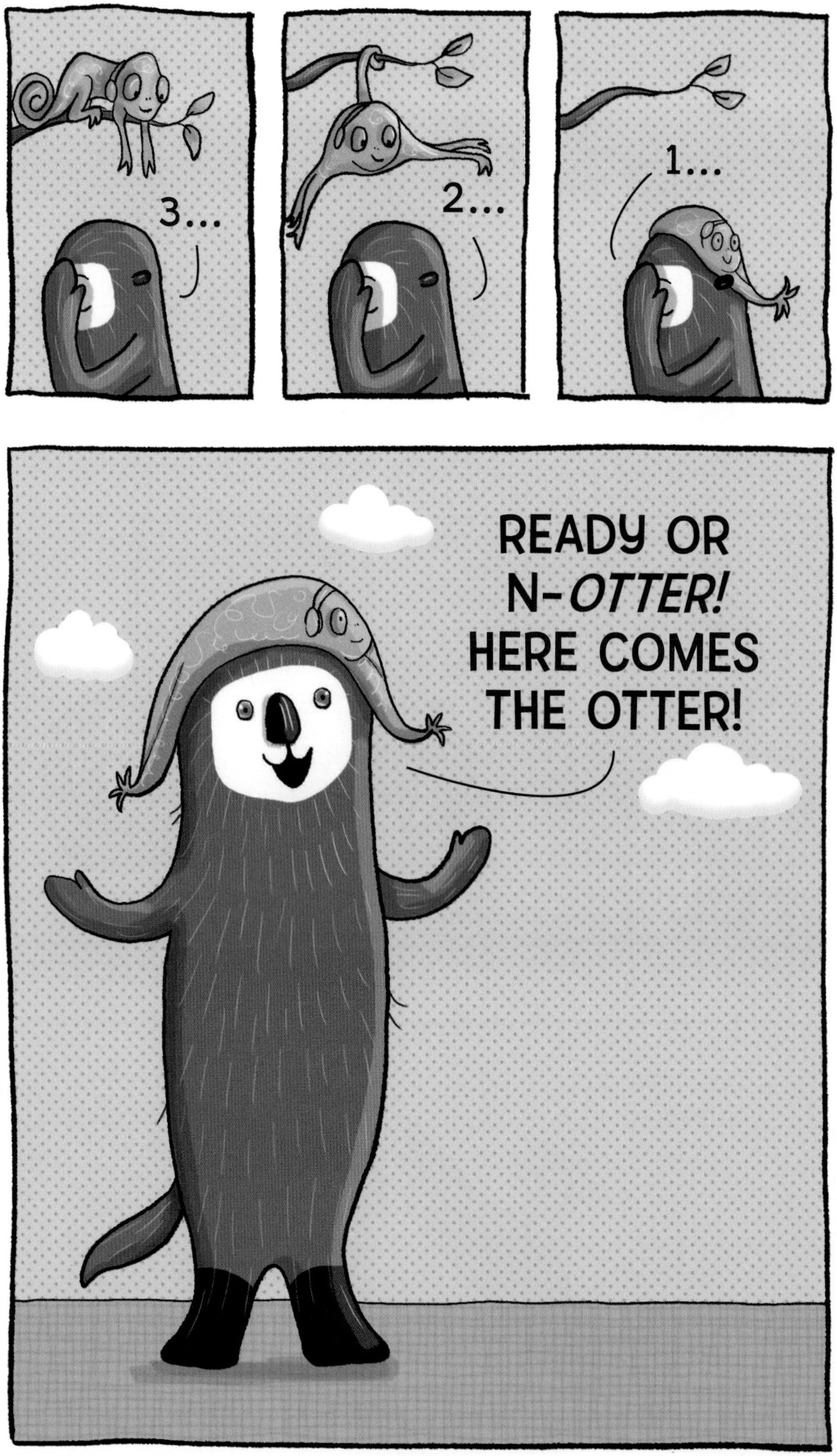
3...
2...
1...
READY OR N-*OTTER!* HERE COMES THE OTTER!

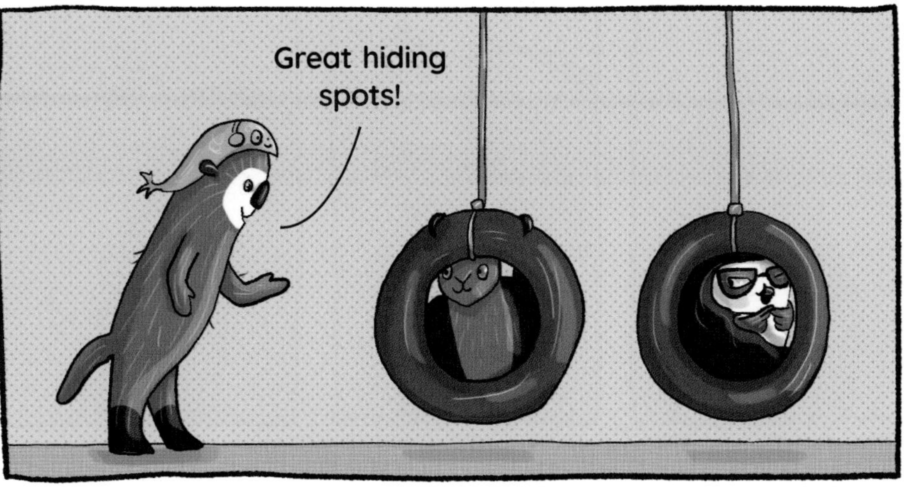
Great hiding spots!

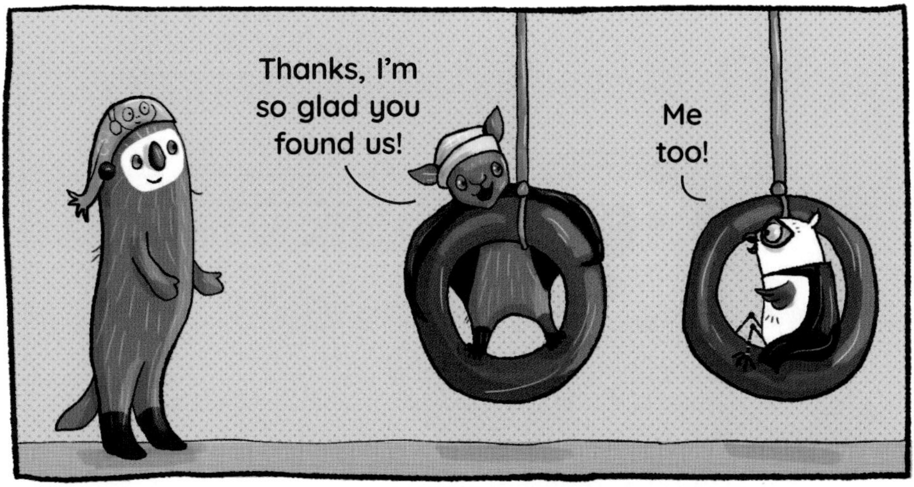
Thanks, I'm so glad you found us!
Me too!

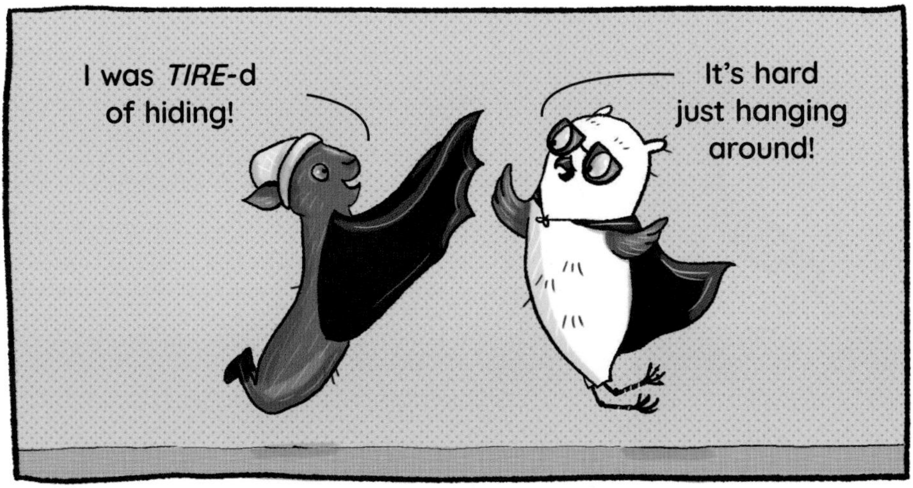
I was *TIRE*-d of hiding!
It's hard just hanging around!

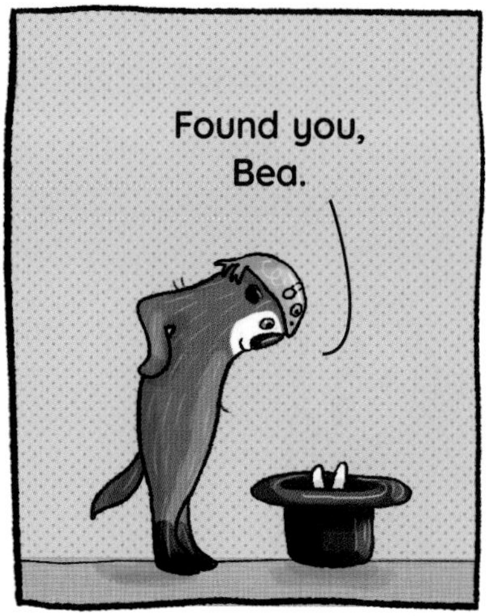
Found you, Bea.

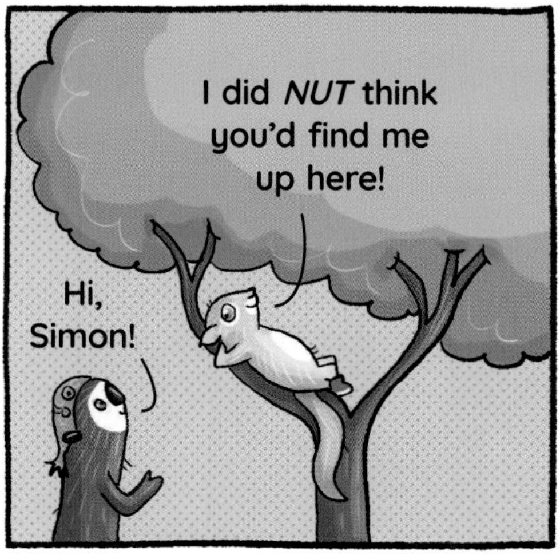
I did *NUT* think you'd find me up here!
Hi, Simon!

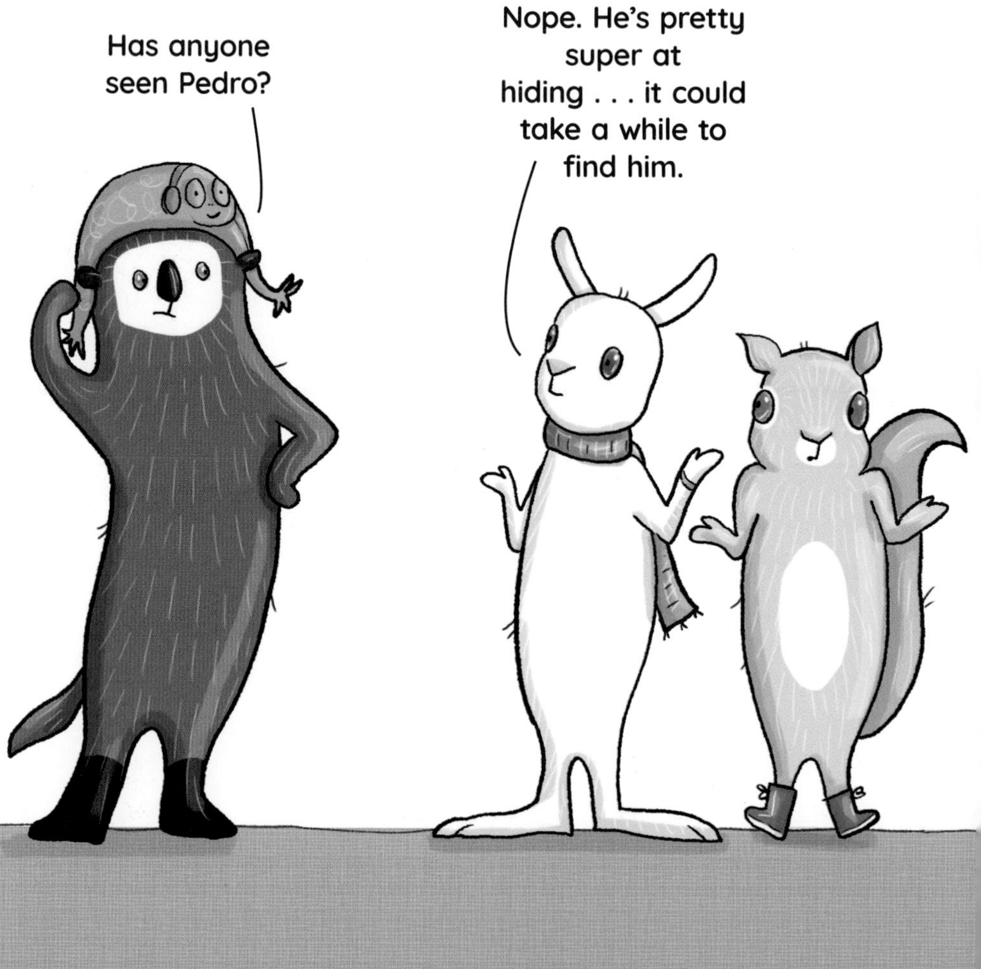
Has anyone seen Pedro?
Nope. He's pretty super at hiding . . . it could take a while to find him.

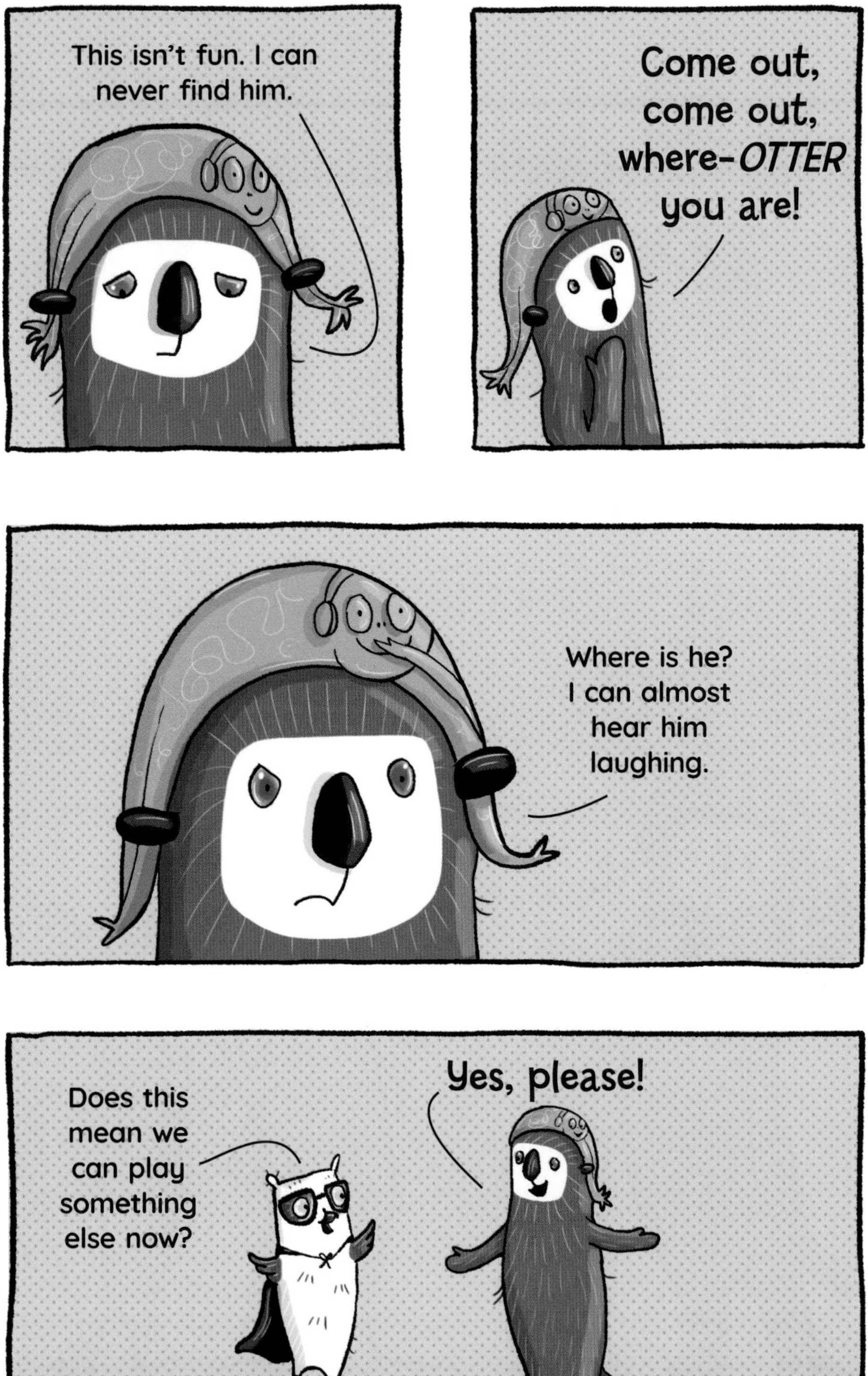
This isn't fun. I can never find him.
Come out, come out, where-*OTTER* you are!
Where is he? I can almost hear him laughing.
Does this mean we can play something else now?
Yes, please!

¡HOLA!
HERE I AM!
YOU DIDN'T FIND ME!
I WIN AGAIN!!!
I TRICKED YOU ALL!

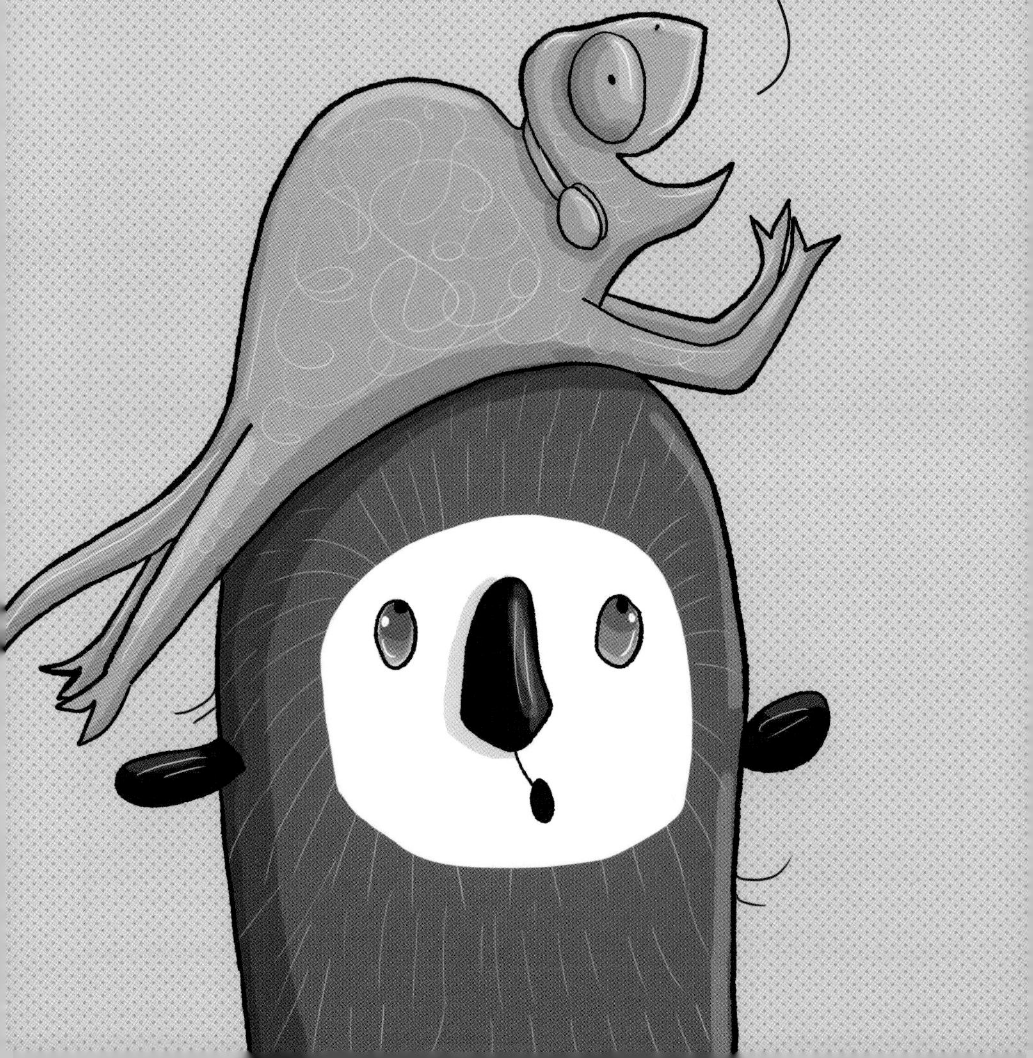

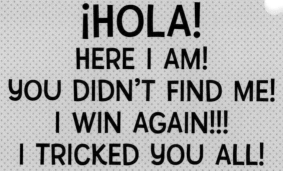

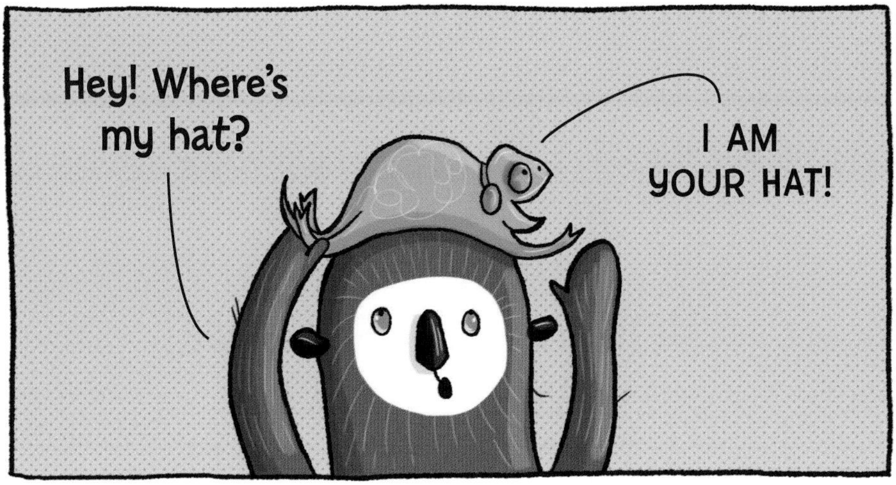
Hey! Where's my hat?
I AM YOUR HAT!

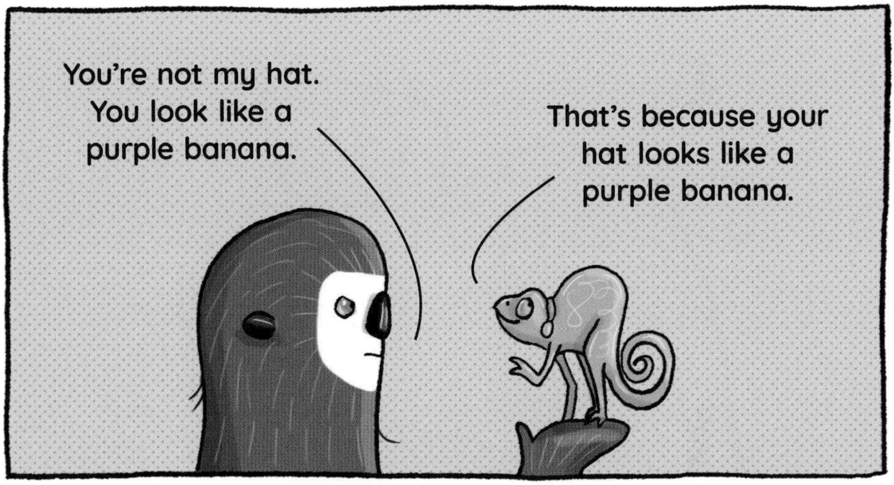
You're not my hat. You look like a purple banana.
That's because your hat looks like a purple banana.

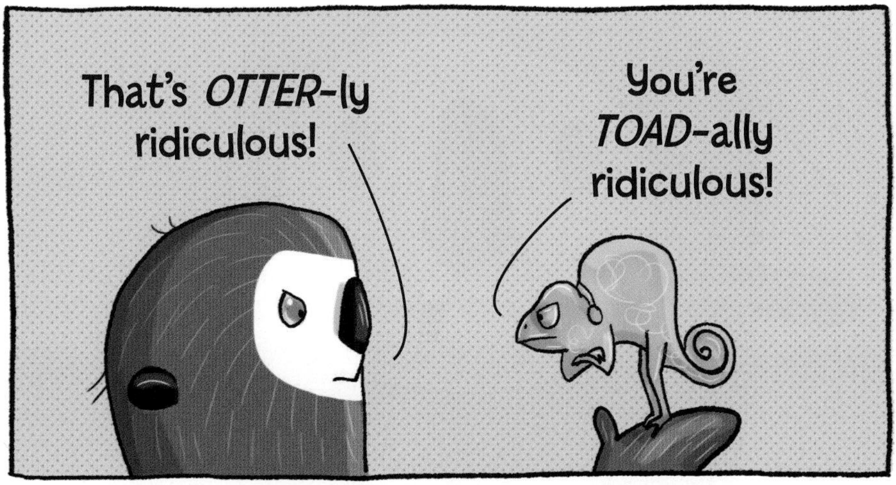
That's *OTTER*-ly ridiculous!
You're *TOAD*-ally ridiculous!

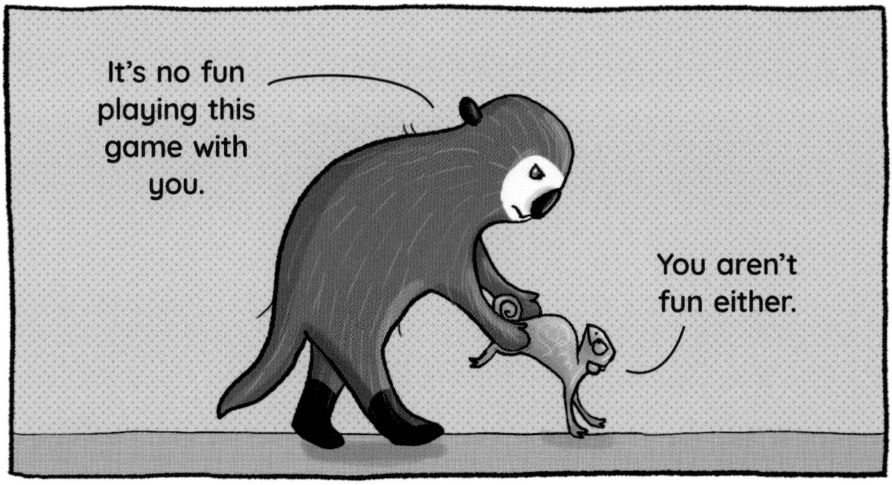
It's no fun playing this game with you.
You aren't fun either.

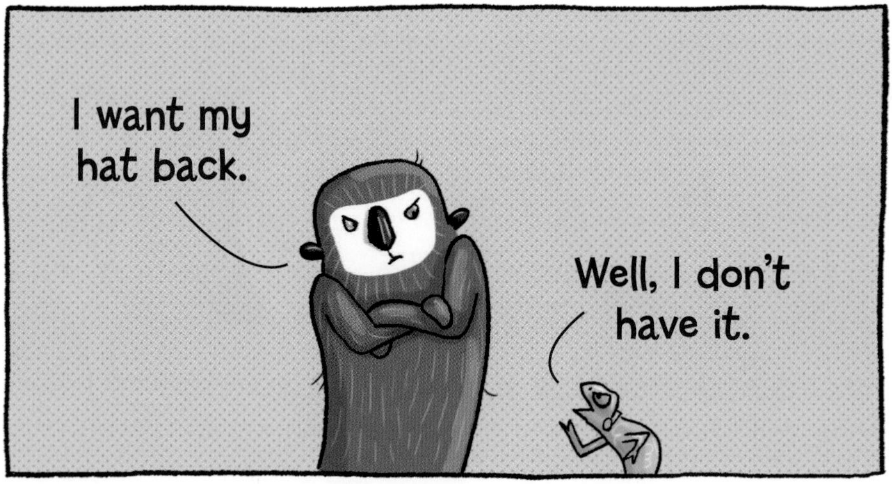
I want my hat back.
Well, I don't have it.

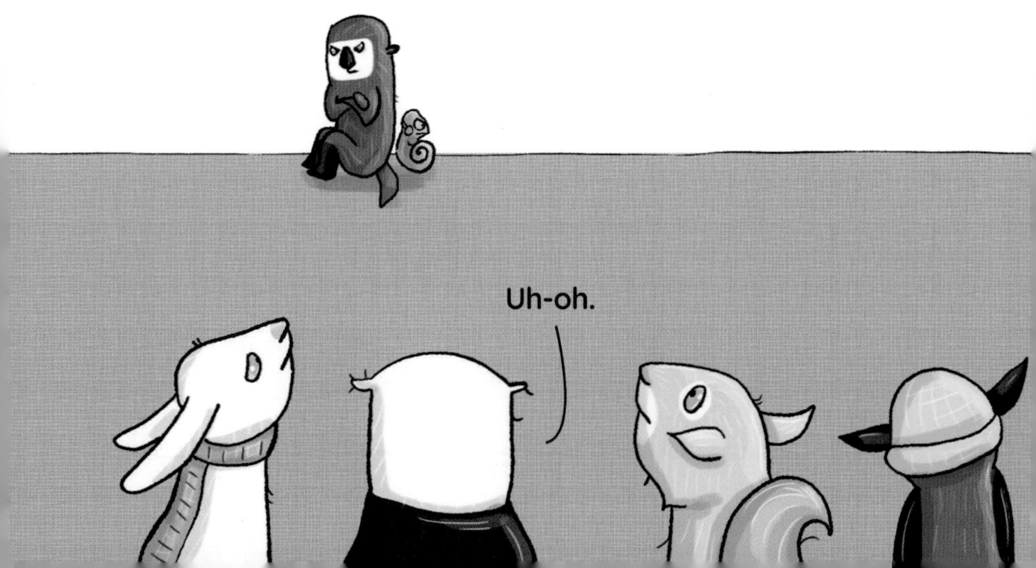
Uh-oh.

CHAPTER 4
DON'T GIVE A HOOT

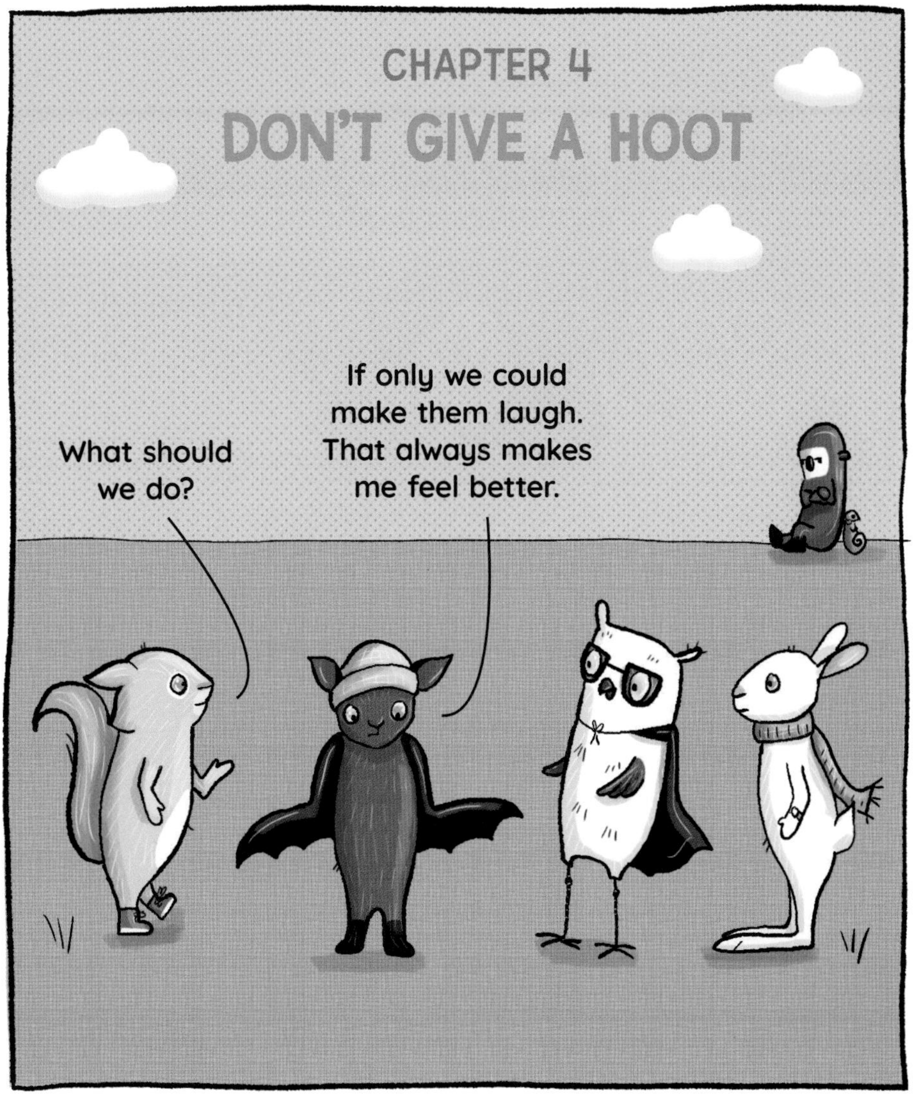
What should we do?
If only we could make them laugh. That always makes me feel better.

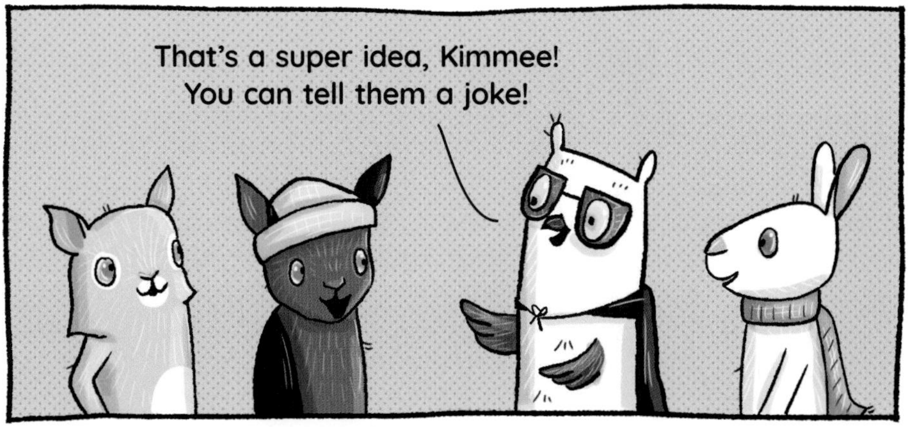
That's a super idea, Kimmee! You can tell them a joke!

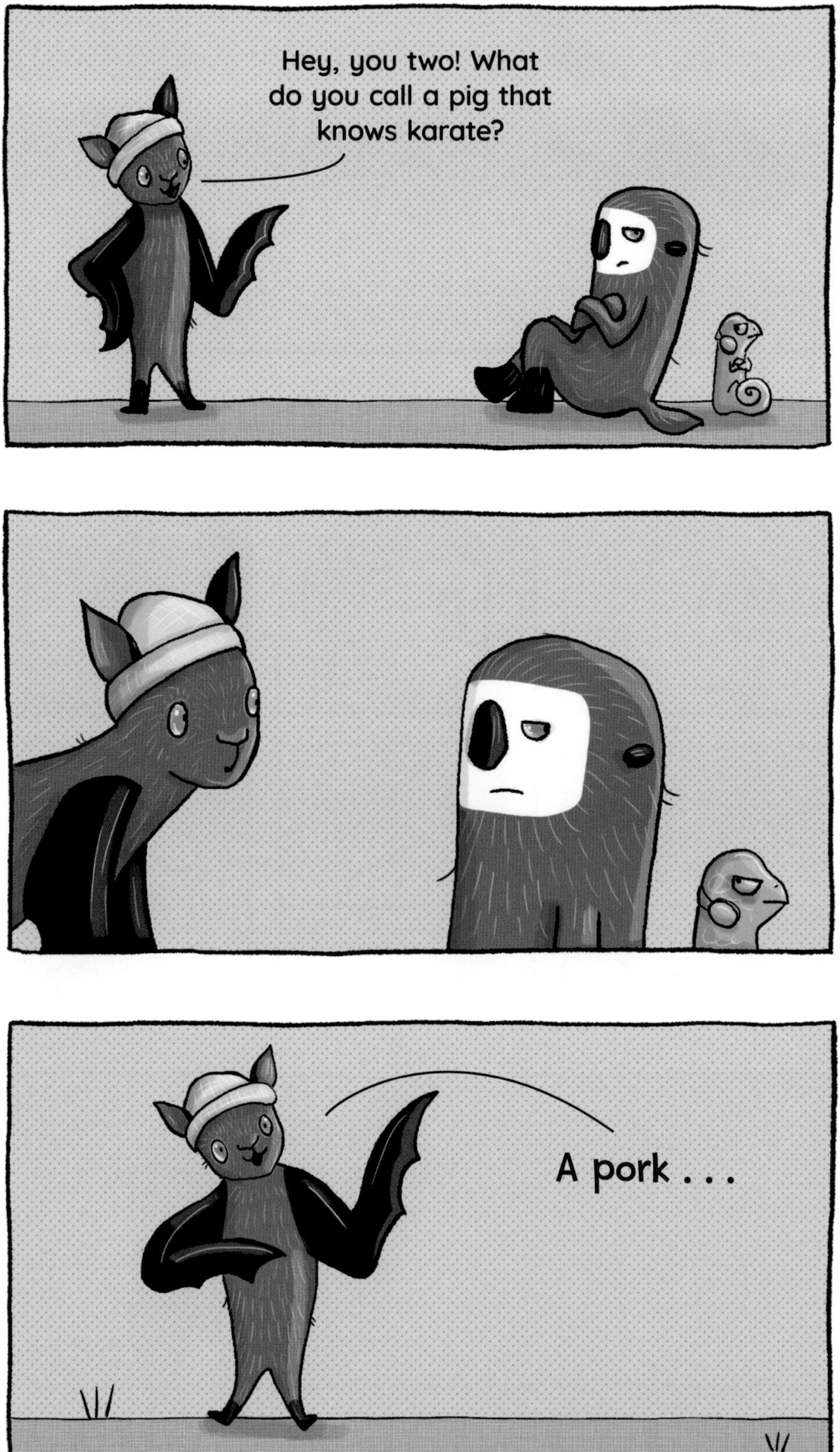
Hey, you two! What do you call a pig that knows karate?
A pork . . .

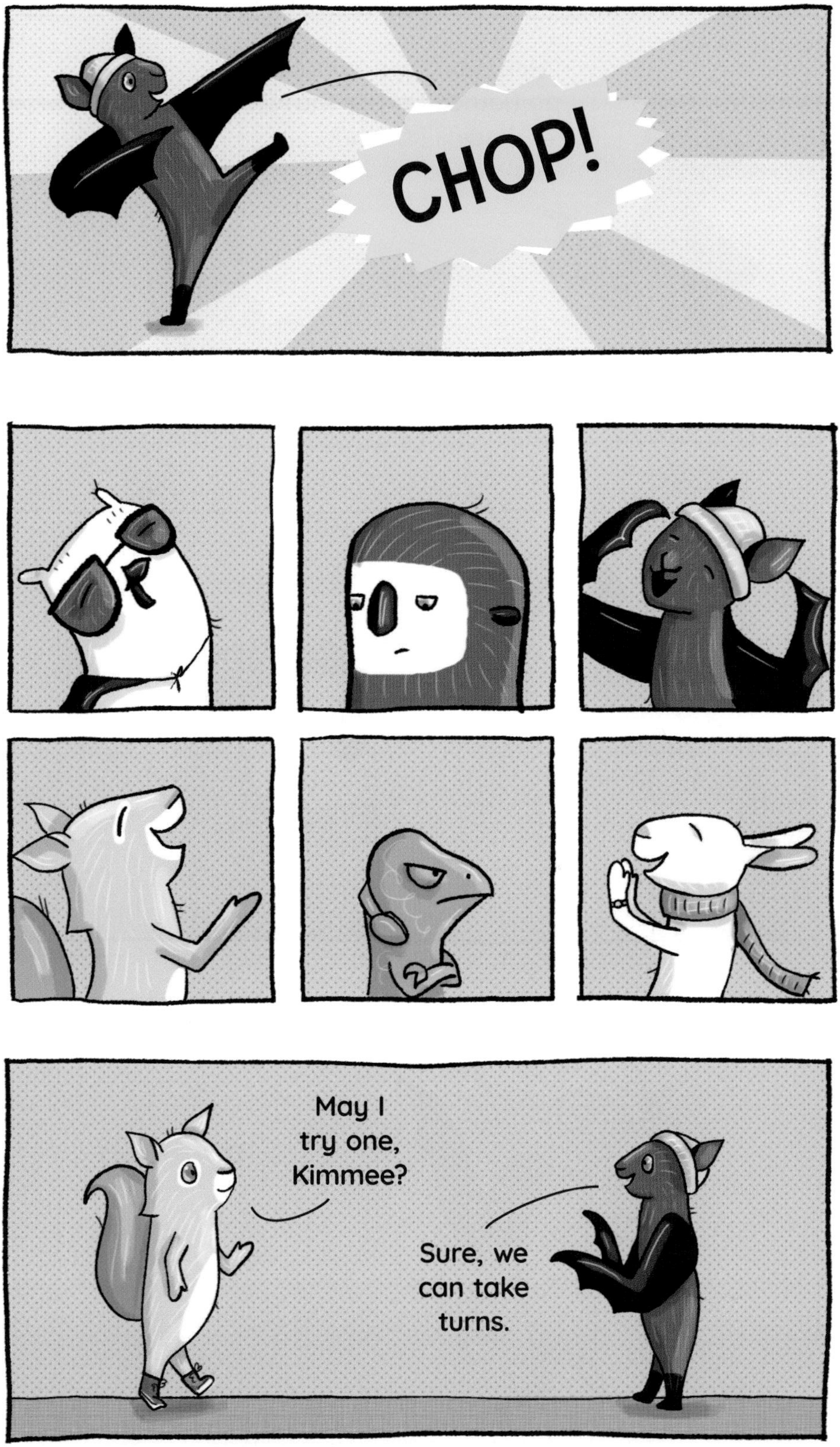
CHOP!
May I try one, Kimmee?
Sure, we can take turns.

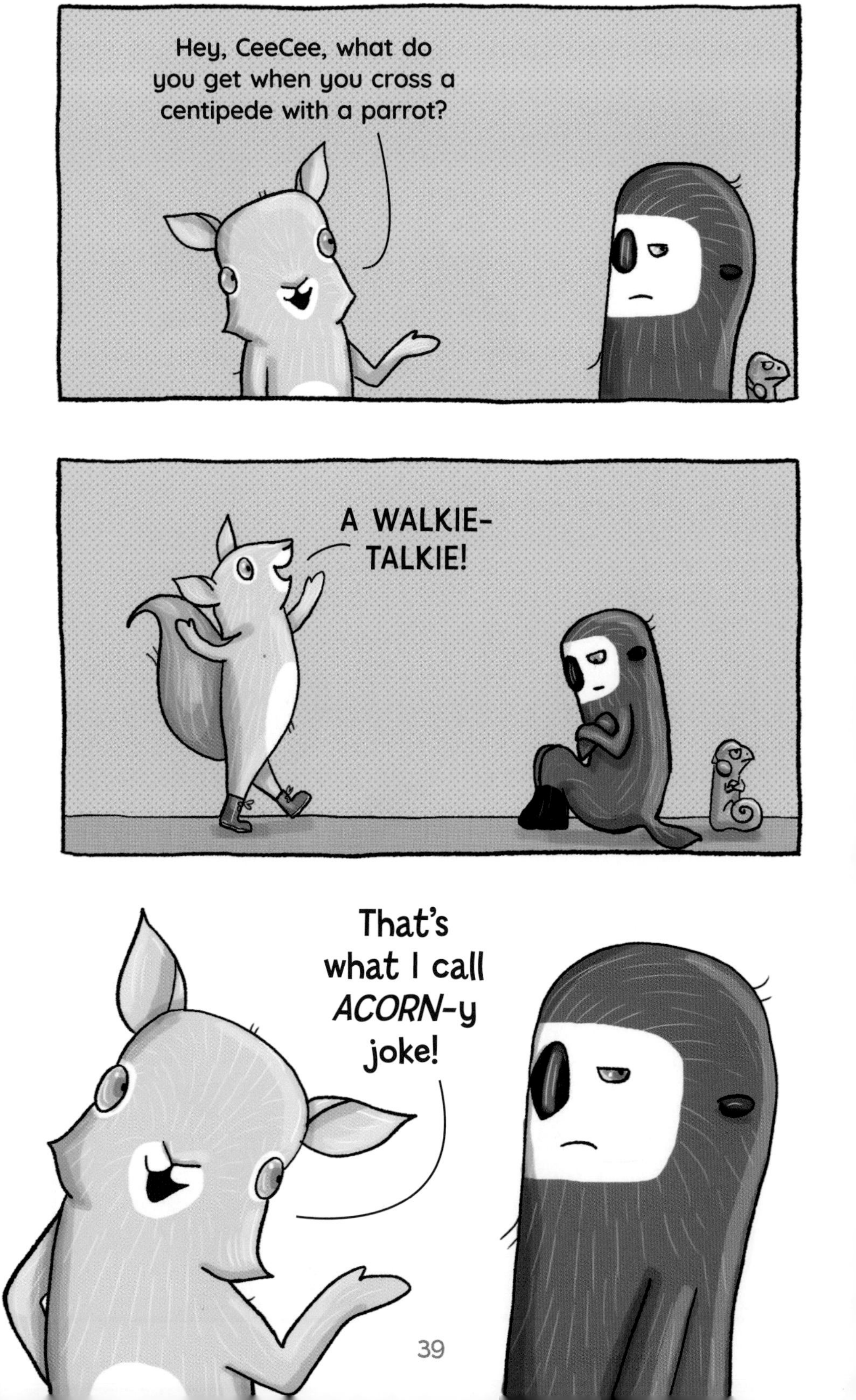
Hey, CeeCee, what do you get when you cross a centipede with a parrot?
A WALKIE-TALKIE!
That's what I call *ACORN*-y joke!

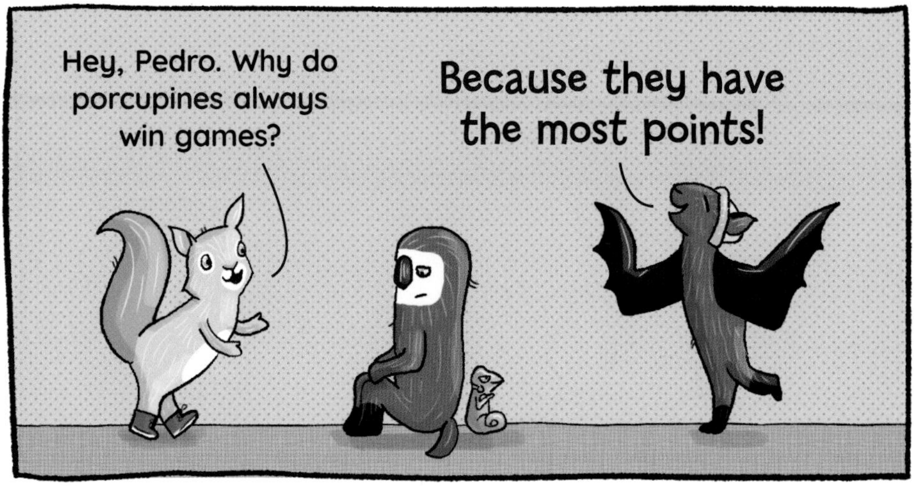
Hey, Pedro. Why do porcupines always win games?
Because they have the most points!

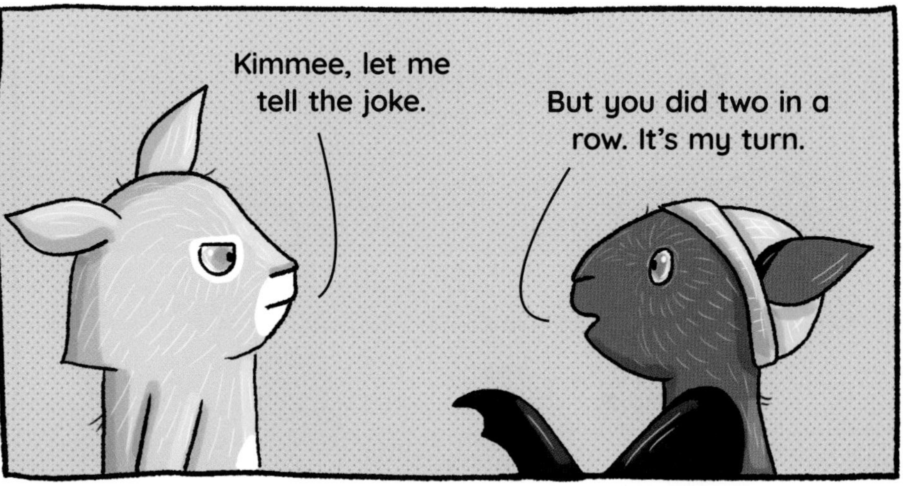
Kimmee, let me tell the joke.
But you did two in a row. It's my turn.

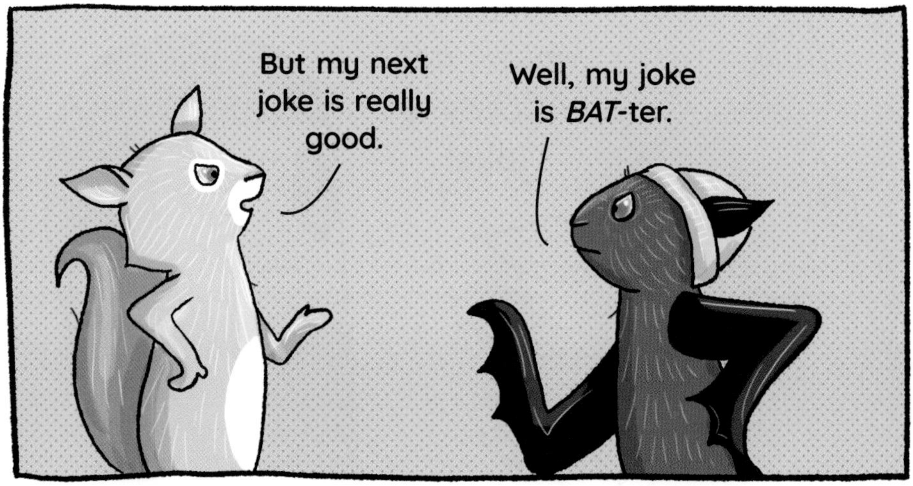
But my next joke is really good.
Well, my joke is *BAT*-ter.

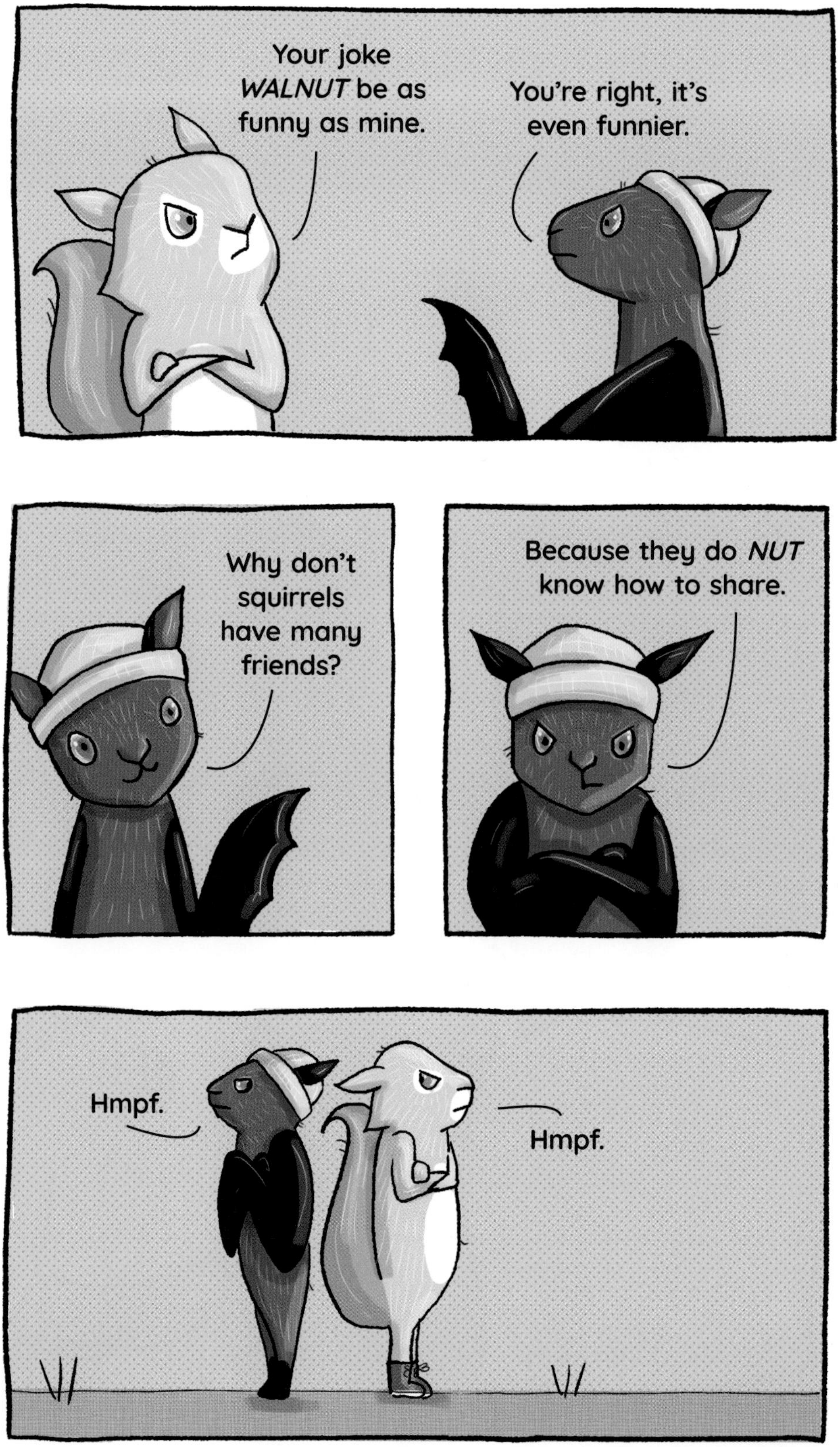
Your joke *WALNUT* be as funny as mine.
You're right, it's even funnier.
Why don't squirrels have many friends?
Because they do *NUT* know how to share.
Hmpf.
Hmpf.

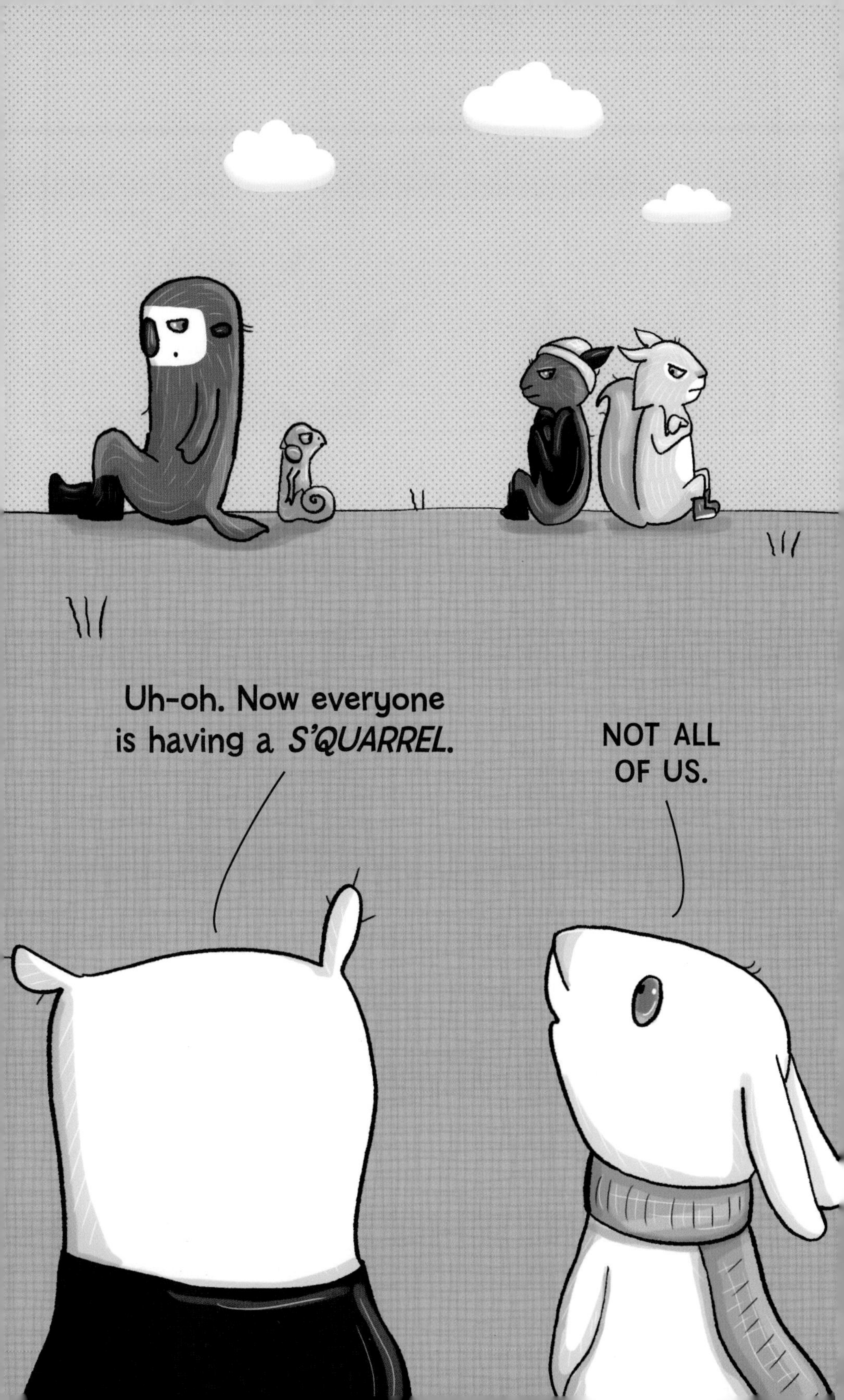
Uh-oh. Now everyone is having a *S'QUARREL*.
NOT ALL OF US.

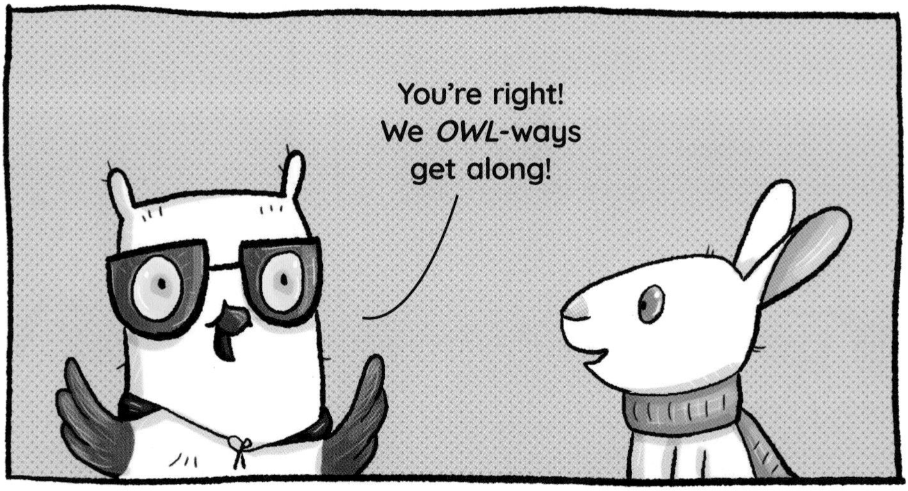
You're right! We *OWL*-ways get along!

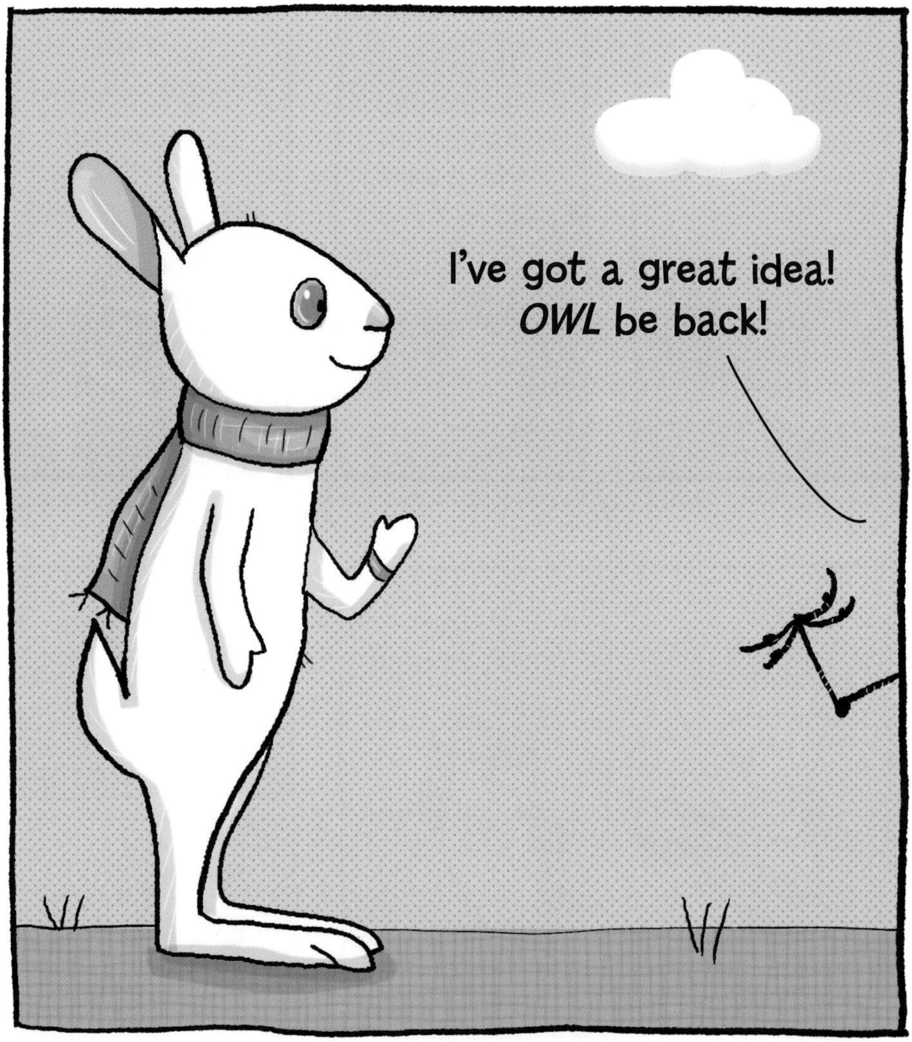
I've got a great idea! *OWL* be back!

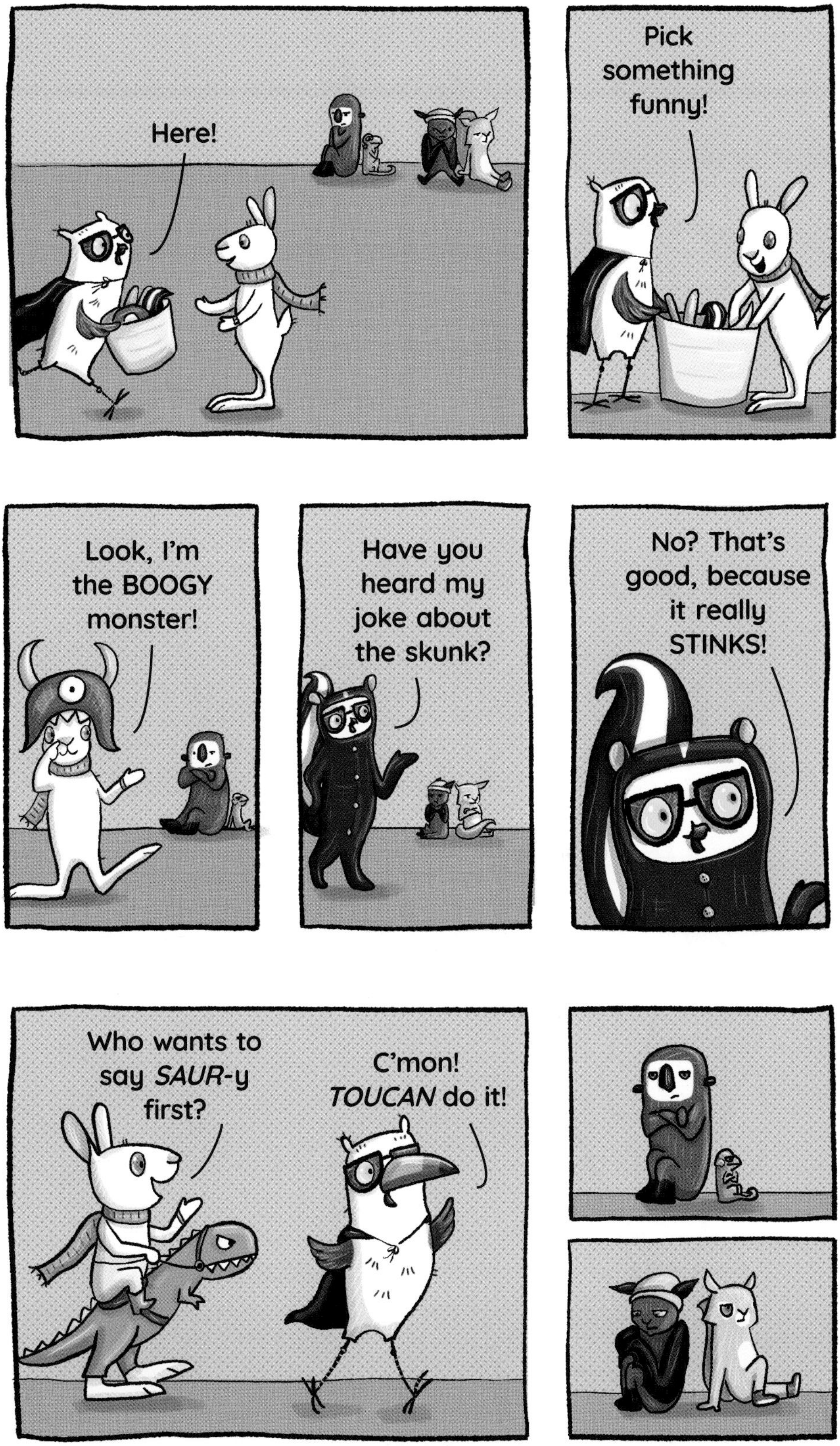
Here!
Pick something funny!
Look, I'm the BOOGY monster!
Have you heard my joke about the skunk?
No? That's good, because it really STINKS!
Who wants to say *SAUR*-y first?
C'mon! *TOUCAN* do it!

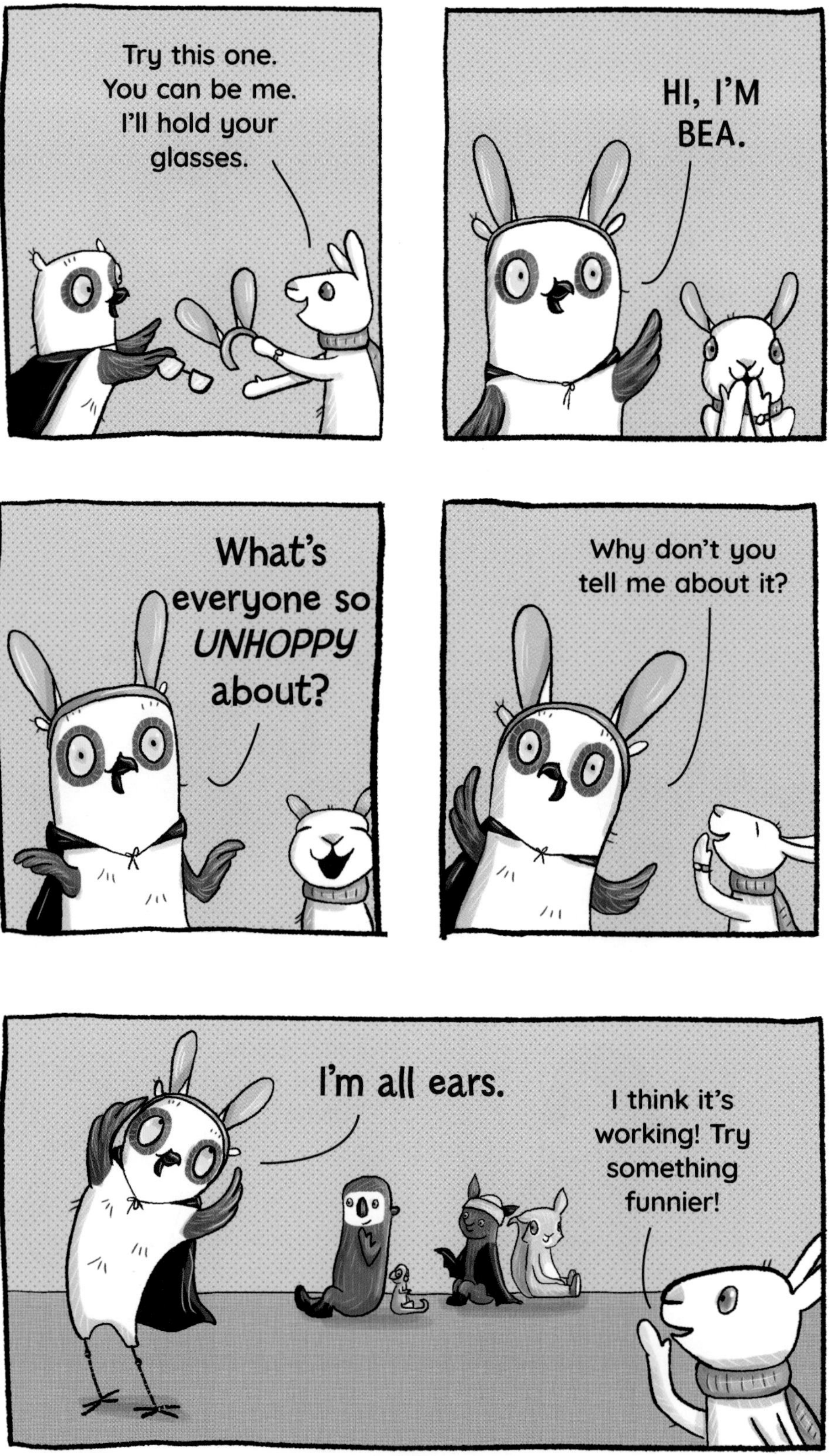
Try this one. You can be me. I'll hold your glasses.
HI, I'M BEA.
What's everyone so *UNHOPPY* about?
Why don't you tell me about it?
I'm all ears.
I think it's working! Try something funnier!

Watch me HIP-HOP!

Look at me!
I'm the best!

I'm a
superjumper!

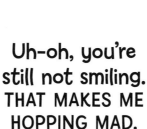

Uh-oh, you're
still not smiling.
THAT MAKES ME
HOPPING MAD.

Time for a
Super Bunny
tantrum!

**THAT'S NOT
BUNNY AT ALL!**

OWL show you
something really
FUNNY!

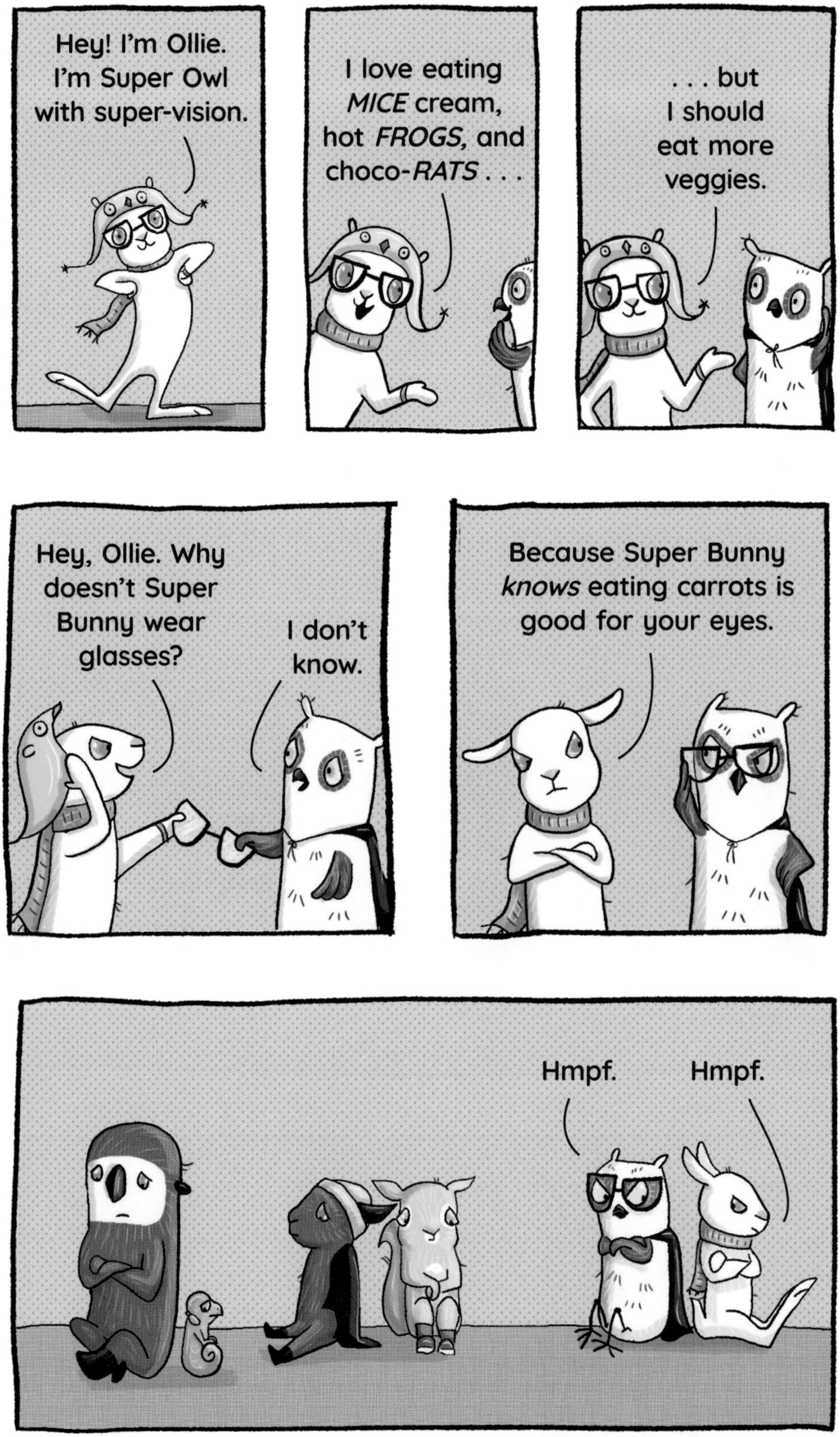

Hey! I'm Ollie. I'm Super Owl with super-vision.
I love eating *MICE* cream, hot *FROGS,* and choco-*RATS* . . .
. . . but I should eat more veggies.
Hey, Ollie. Why doesn't Super Bunny wear glasses?
I don't know.
Because Super Bunny *knows* eating carrots is good for your eyes.
Hmpf.
Hmpf.

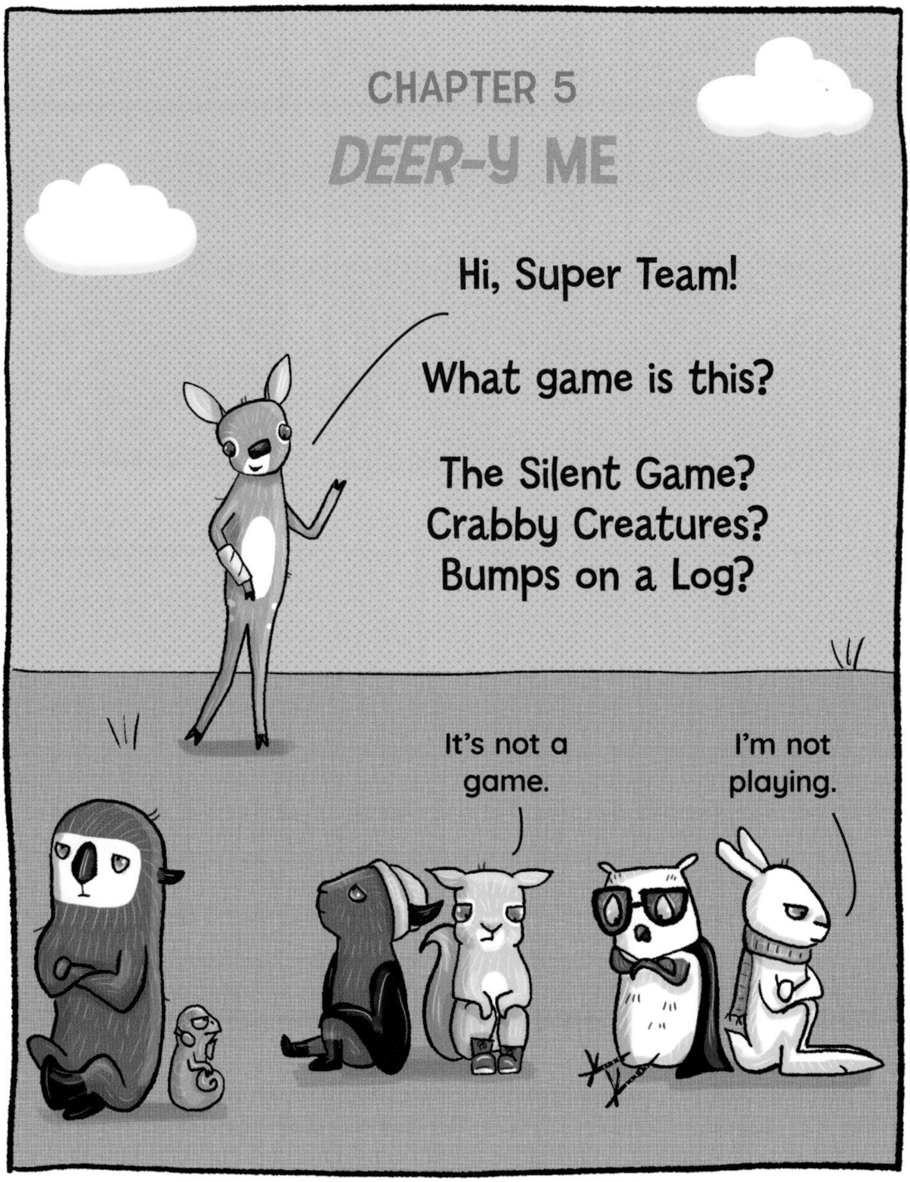
CHAPTER 5
DEER-Y ME
Hi, Super Team!
What game is this?
The Silent Game?
Crabby Creatures?
Bumps on a Log?
It's not a game.
I'm not playing.

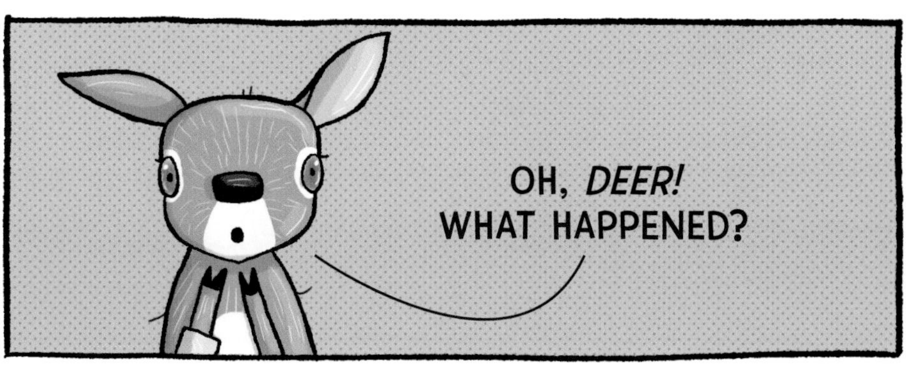
OH, *DEER!*
WHAT HAPPENED?

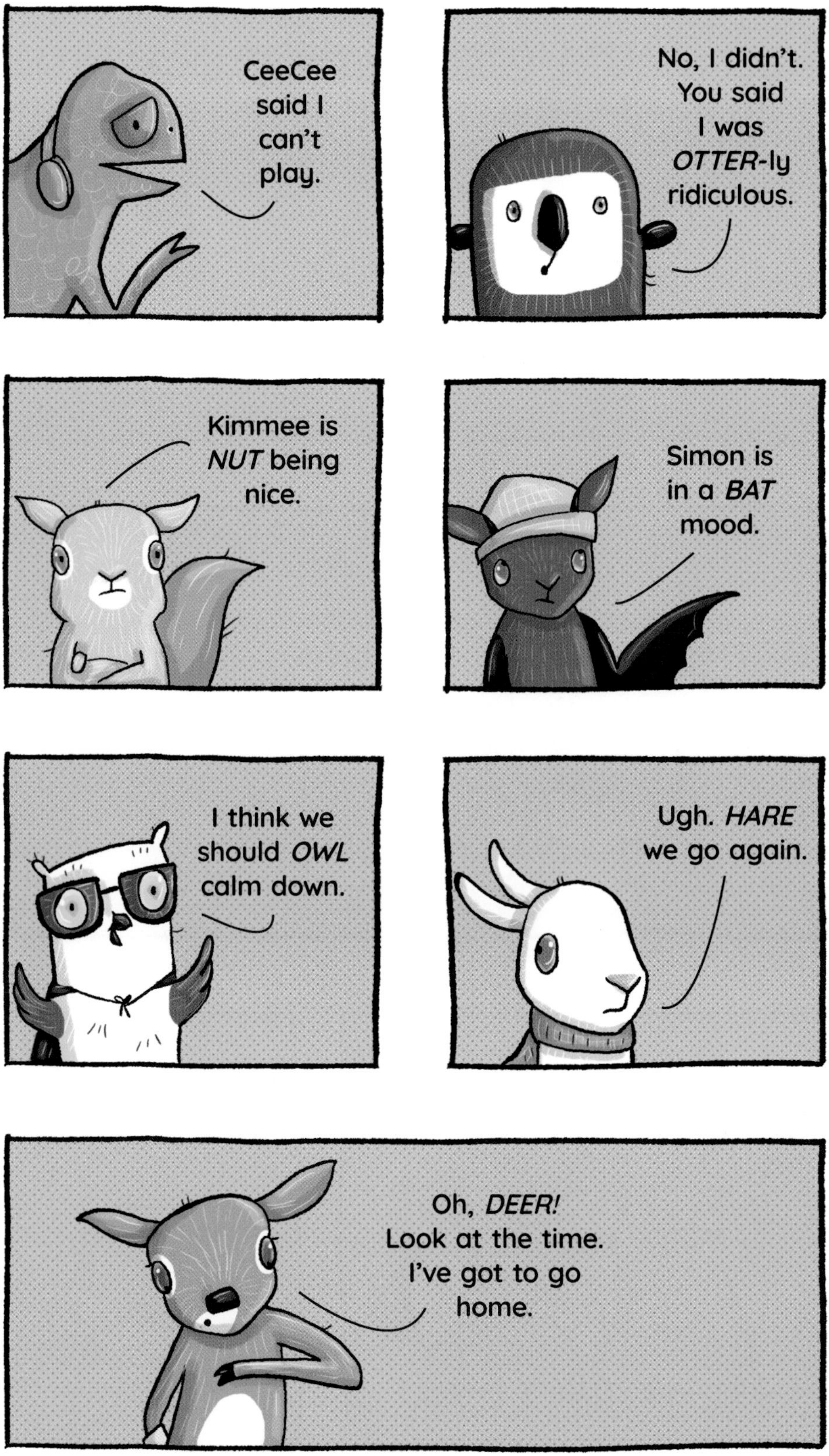
CeeCee said I can't play.
No, I didn't. You said I was *OTTER*-ly ridiculous.
Kimmee is *NUT* being nice.
Simon is in a *BAT* mood.
I think we should *OWL* calm down.
Ugh. *HARE* we go again.
Oh, *DEER!* Look at the time. I've got to go home.

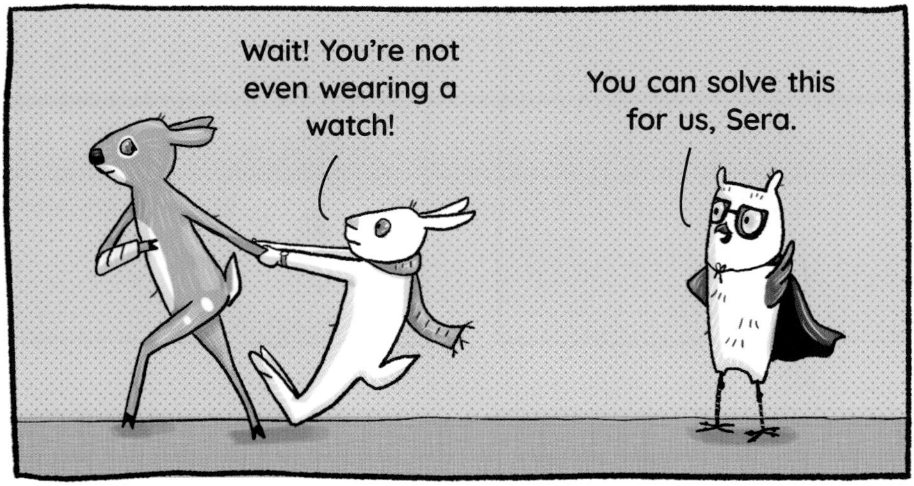
Wait! You're not even wearing a watch!
You can solve this for us, Sera.

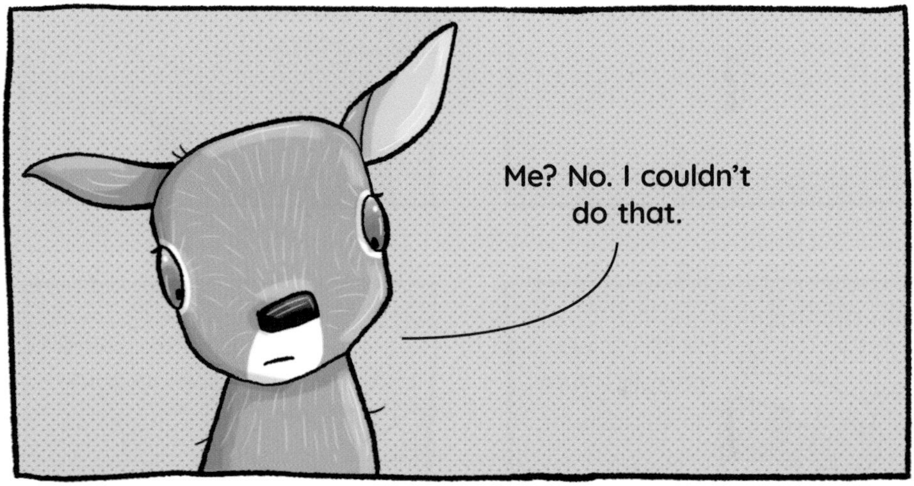
Me? No. I couldn't do that.

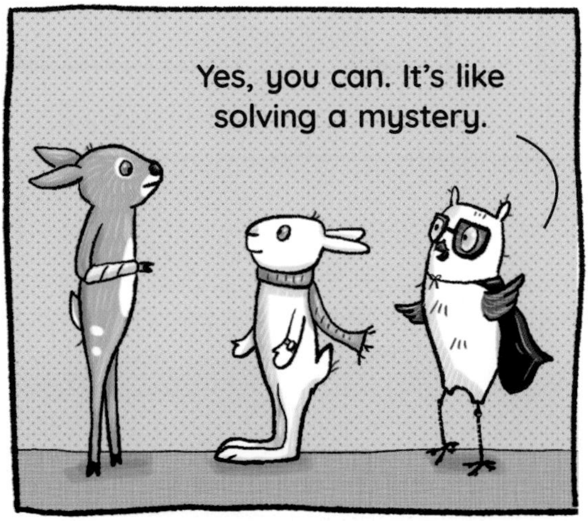
Yes, you can. It's like solving a mystery.

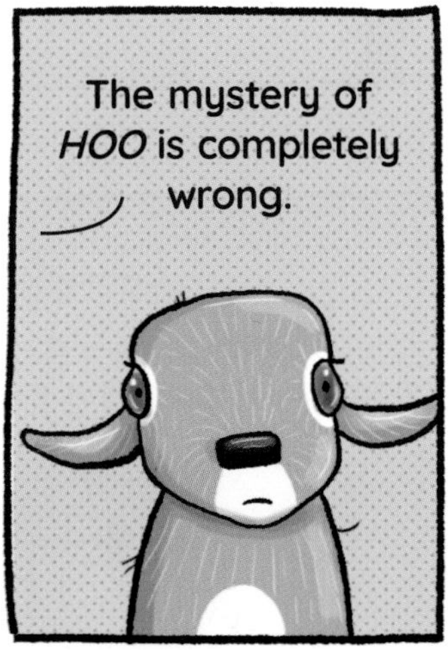
The mystery of *HOO* is completely wrong.

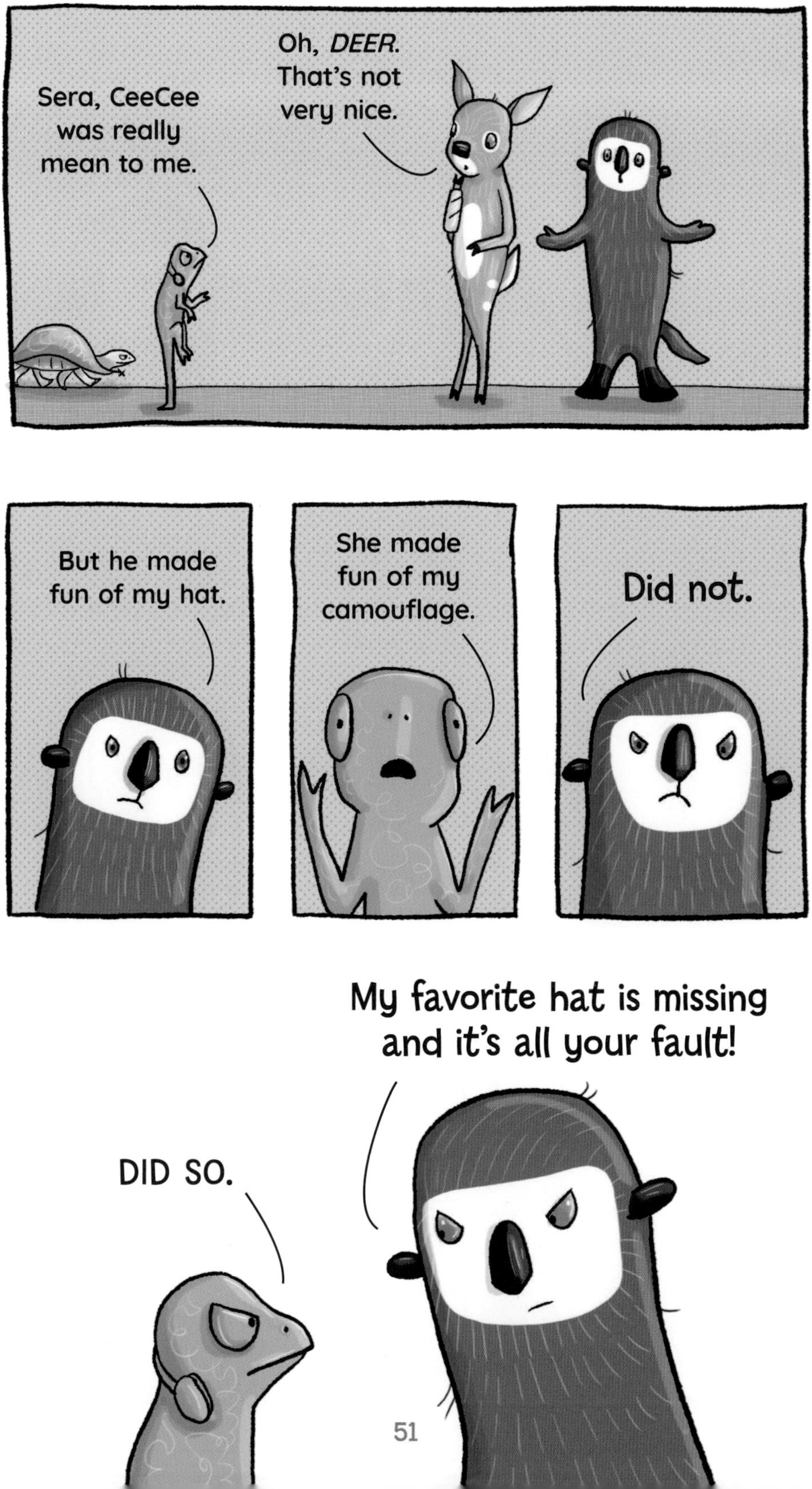
Sera, CeeCee was really mean to me.
Oh, *DEER*. That's not very nice.
But he made fun of my hat.
She made fun of my camouflage.
Did not.
DID SO.
My favorite hat is missing and it's all your fault!

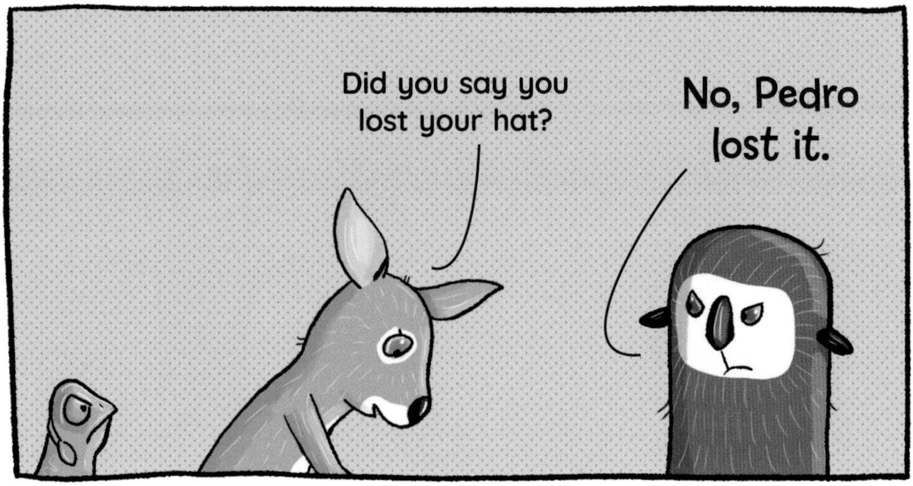
Did you say you lost your hat?
No, Pedro lost it.

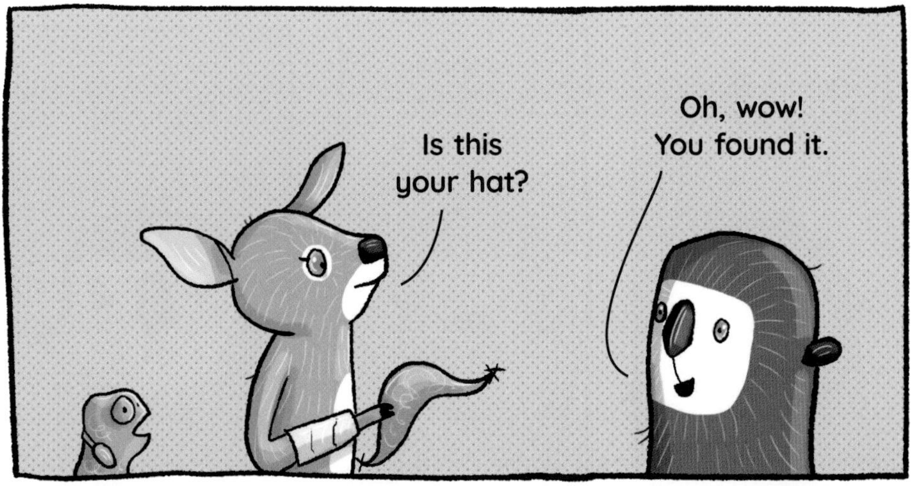
Is this your hat?
Oh, wow! You found it.

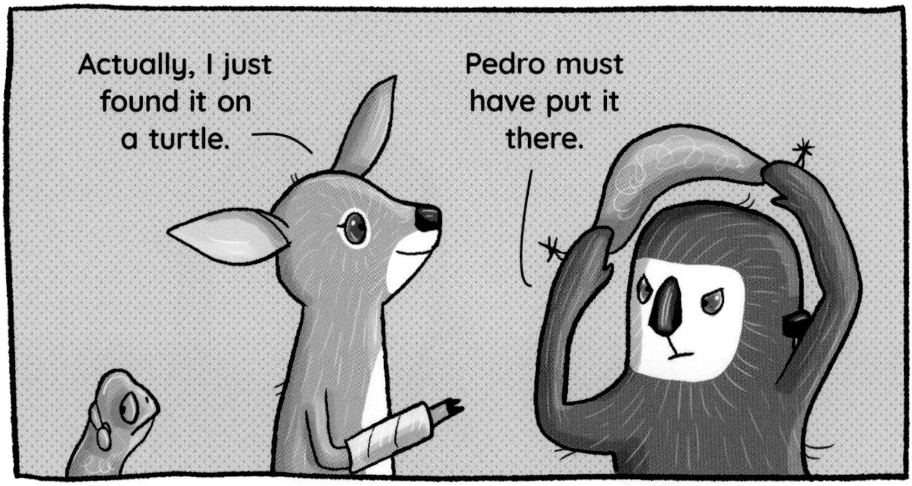
Actually, I just found it on a turtle.
Pedro must have put it there.

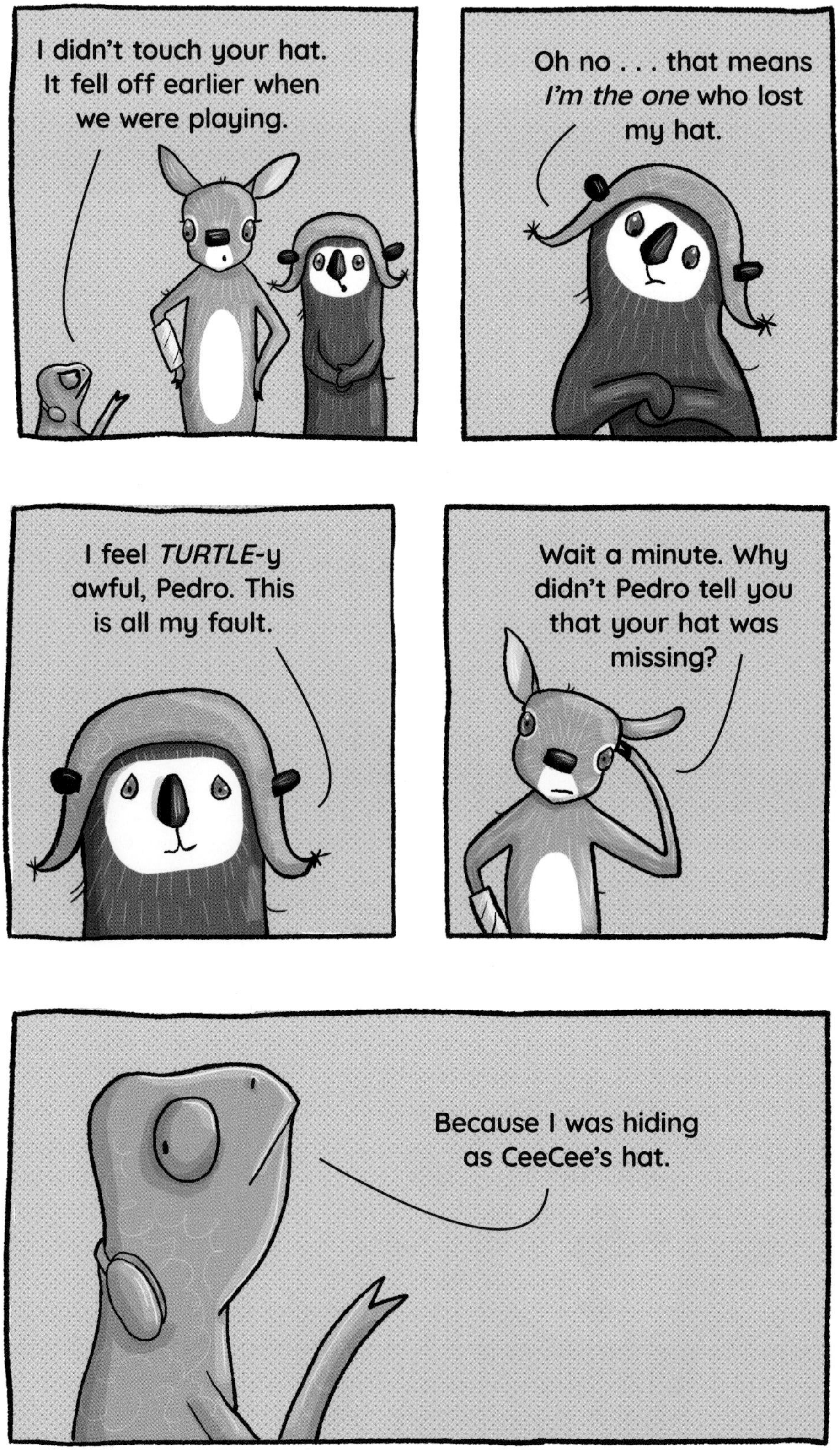
I didn't touch your hat. It fell off earlier when we were playing.
Oh no . . . that means *I'm the one* who lost my hat.
I feel *TURTLE*-y awful, Pedro. This is all my fault.
Wait a minute. Why didn't Pedro tell you that your hat was missing?
Because I was hiding as CeeCee's hat.

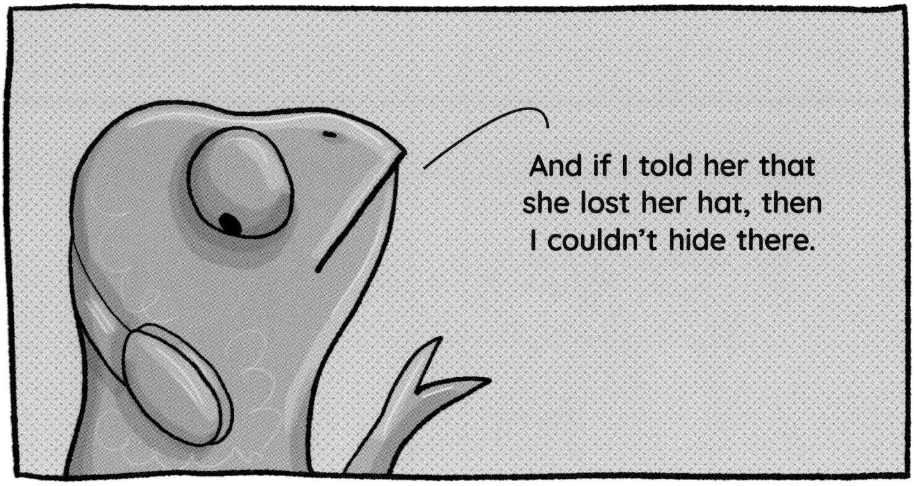
And if I told her that she lost her hat, then I couldn't hide there.

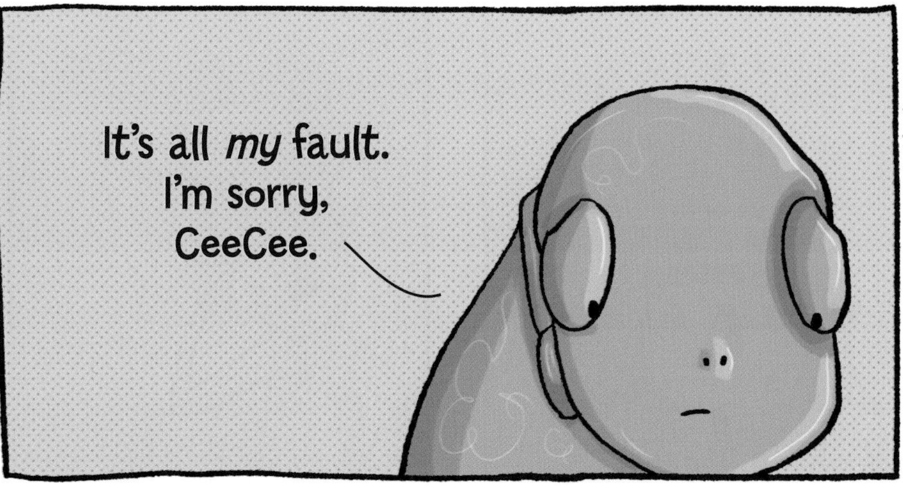
It's all *my* fault. I'm sorry, CeeCee.

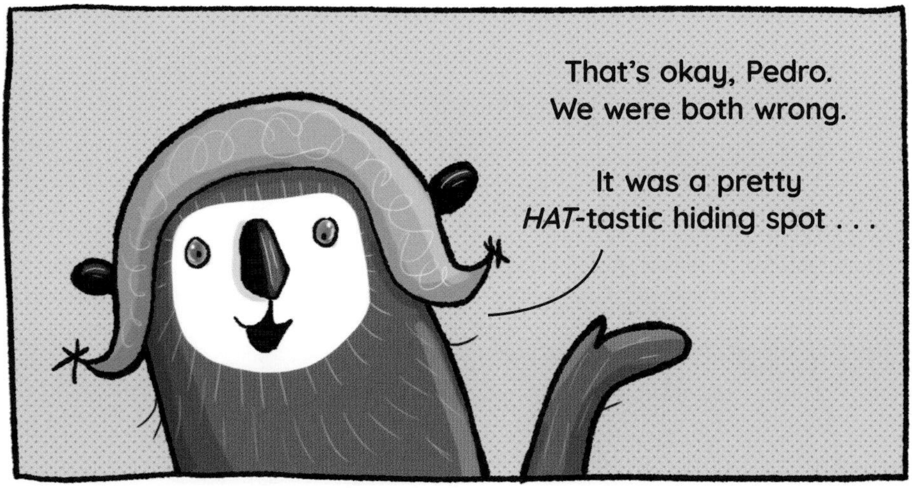
That's okay, Pedro. We were both wrong.
It was a pretty *HAT*-tastic hiding spot . . .

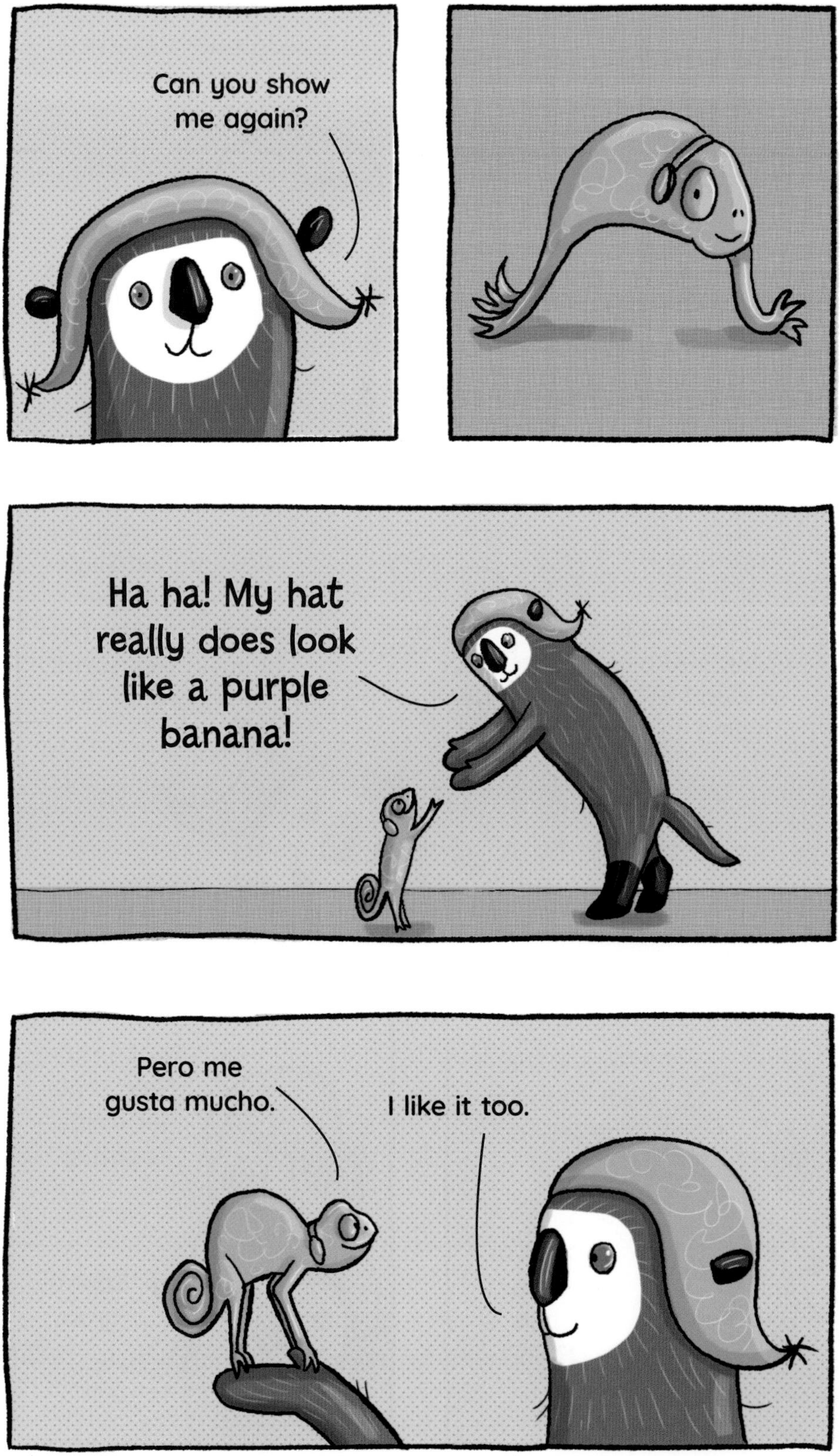
Can you show me again?
Ha ha! My hat really does look like a purple banana!
Pero me gusta mucho.
I like it too.

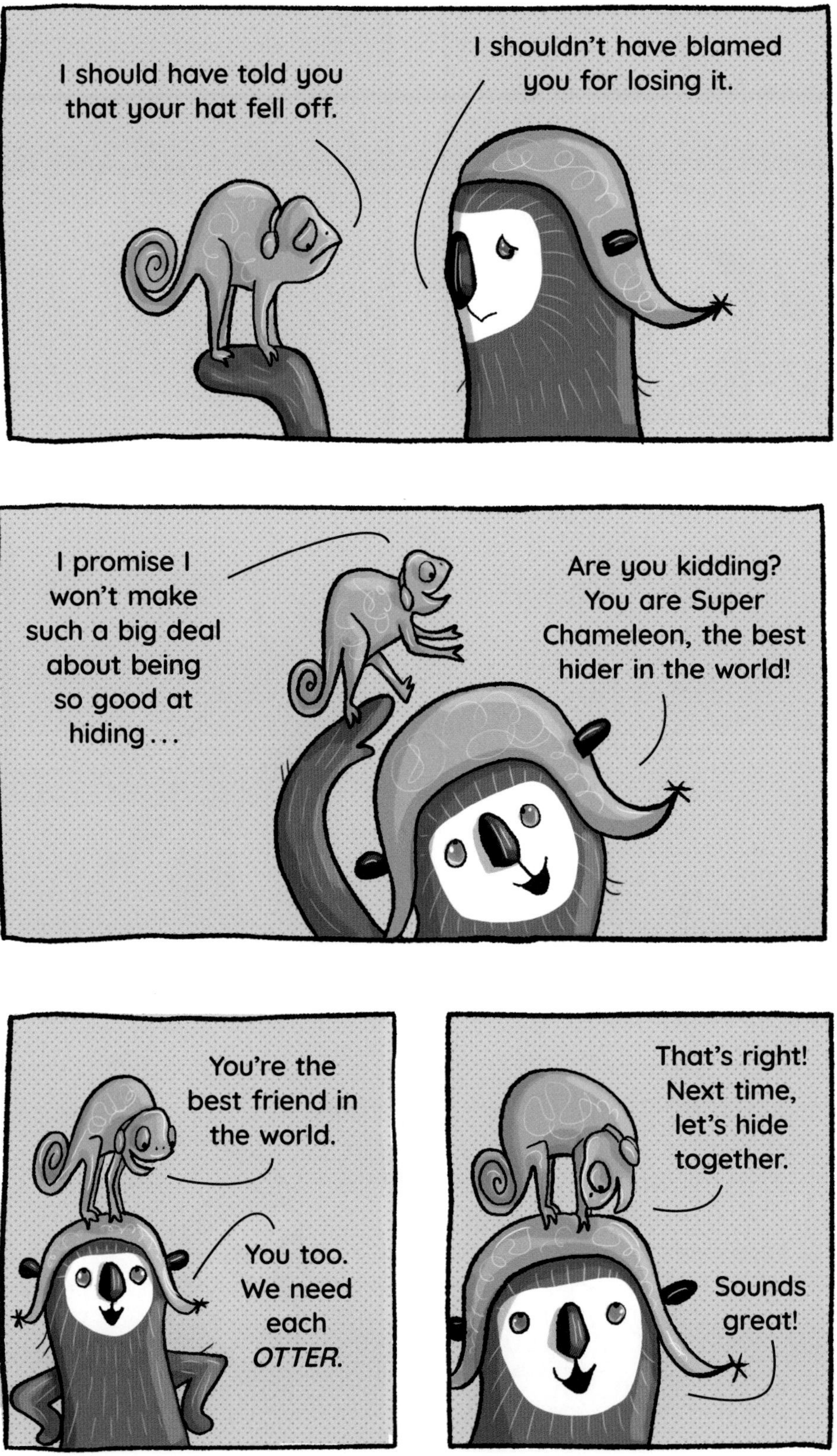
I should have told you that your hat fell off.
I shouldn't have blamed you for losing it.
I promise I won't make such a big deal about being so good at hiding...
Are you kidding? You are Super Chameleon, the best hider in the world!
You're the best friend in the world.
You too. We need each *OTTER*.
That's right! Next time, let's hide together.
Sounds great!

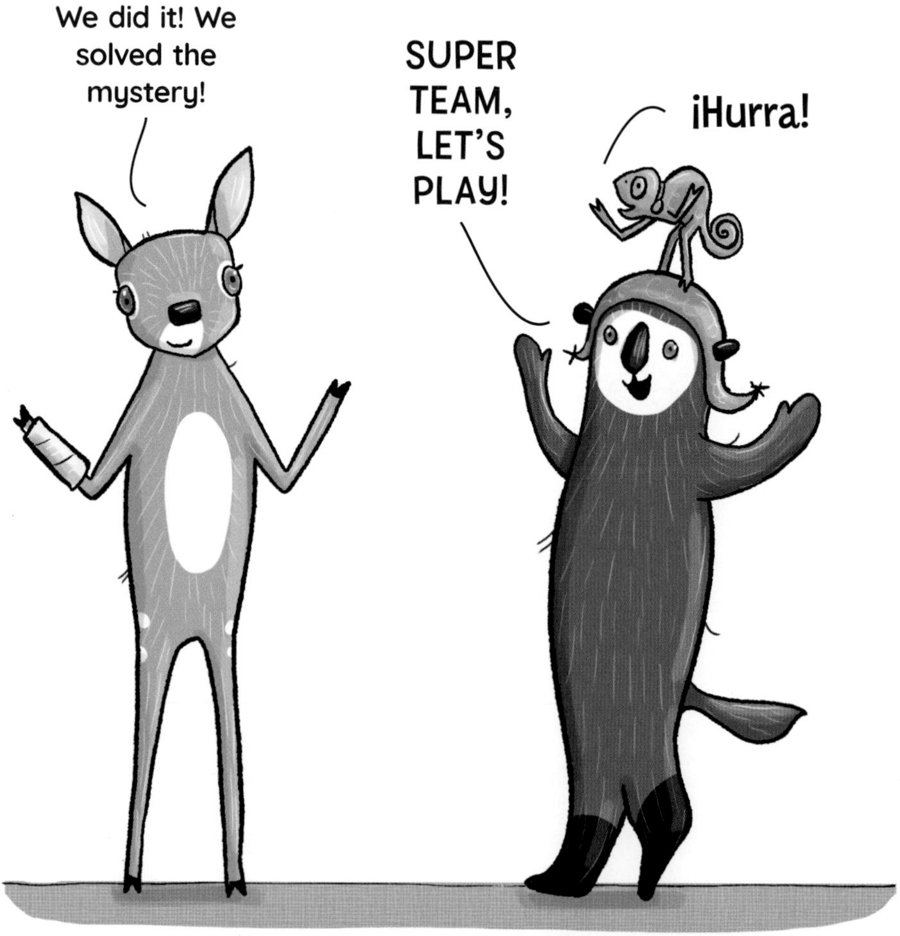
We did it! We solved the mystery!
SUPER TEAM, LET'S PLAY!
¡Hurra!

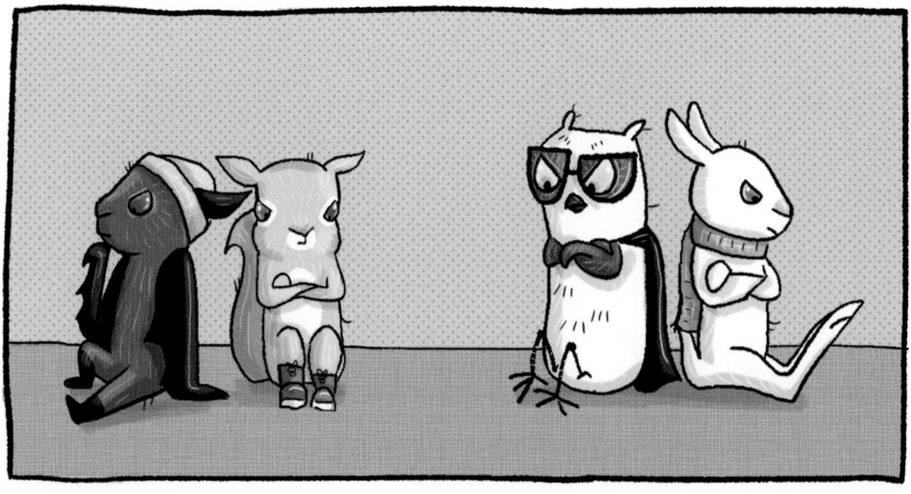

CHAPTER 6

FROG-GIVE AND *FROG*-GET

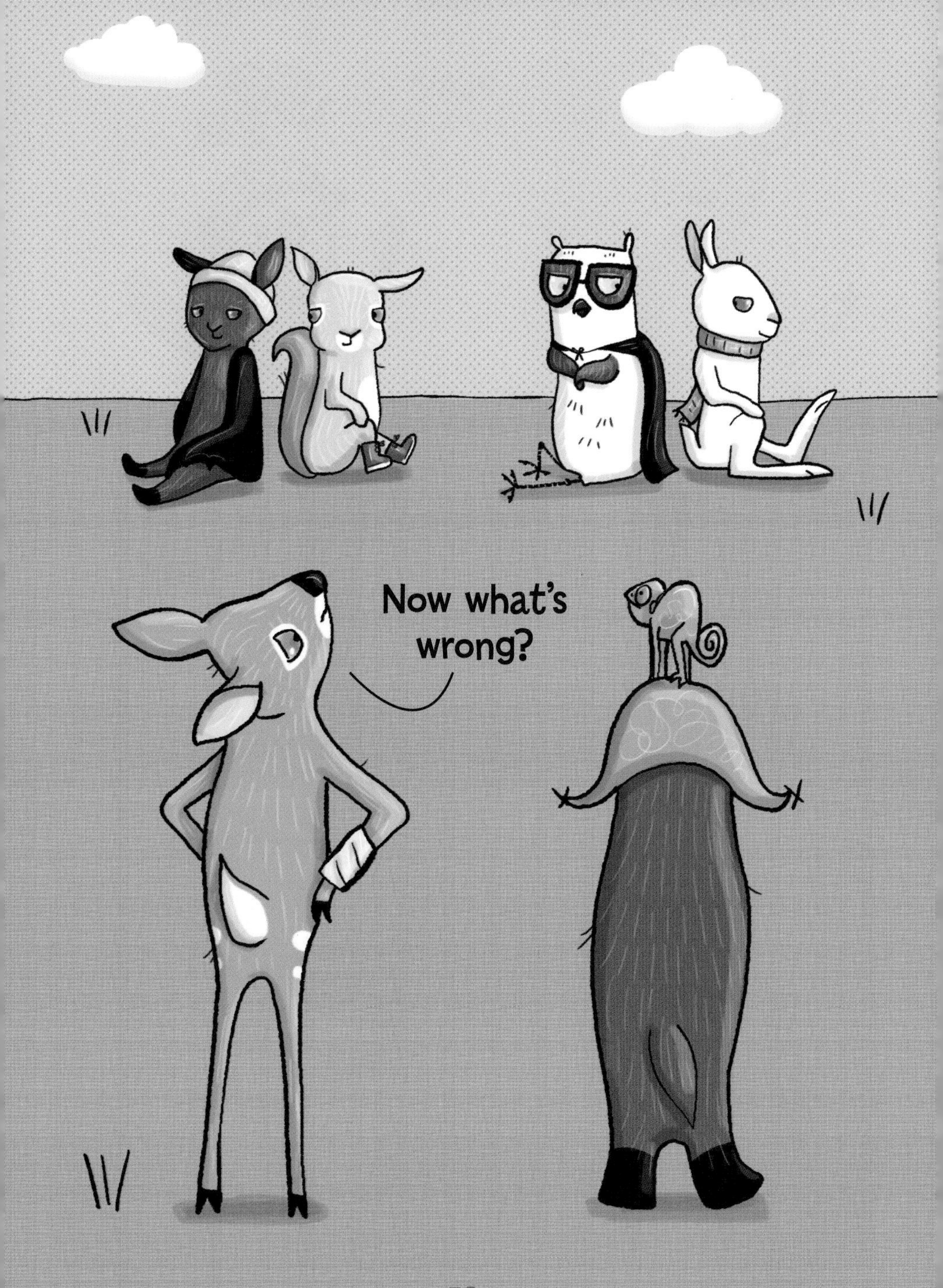
Now what's wrong?

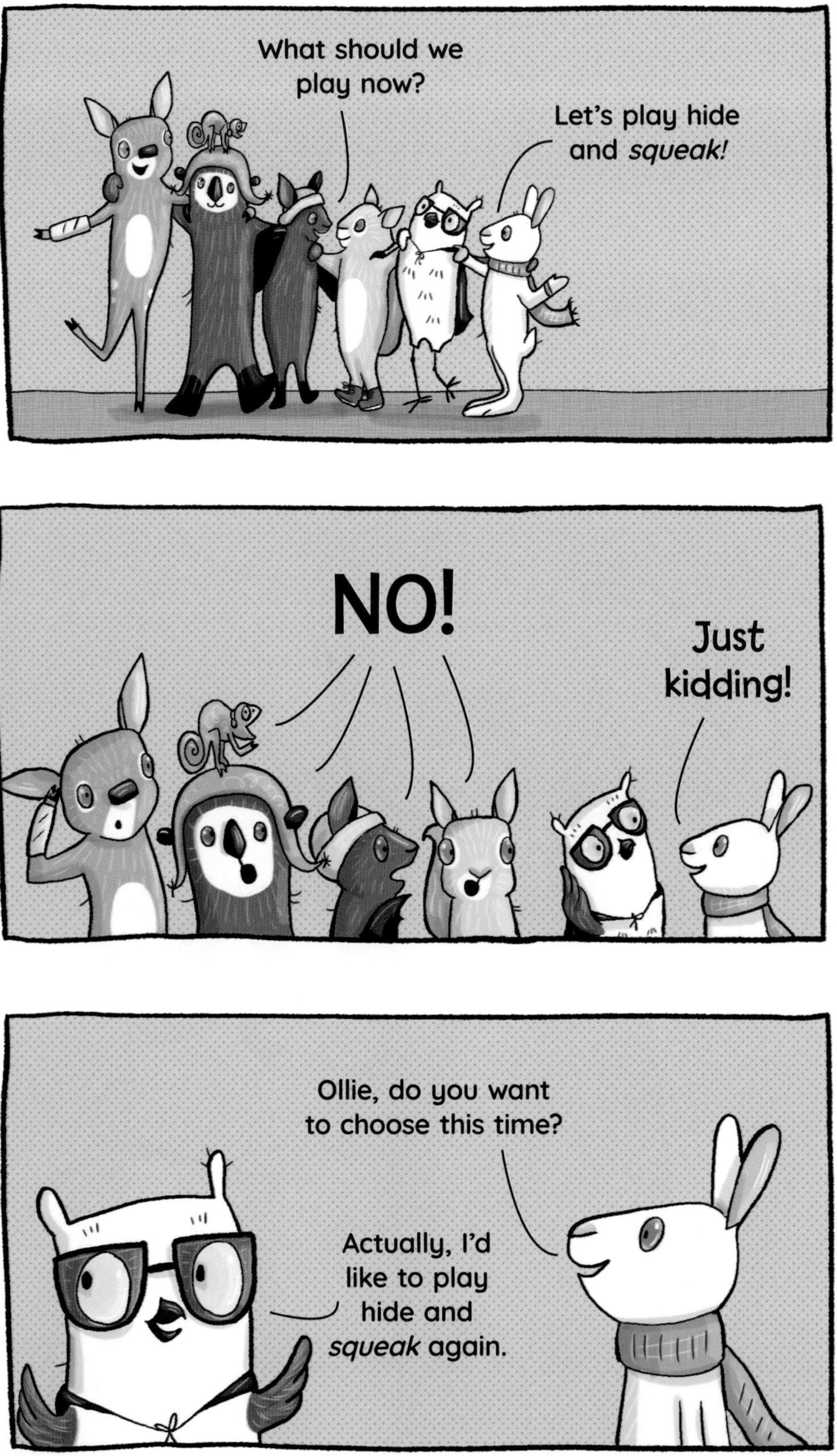
What should we play now?
Let's play hide and *squeak!*
NO!
Just kidding!
Ollie, do you want to choose this time?
Actually, I'd like to play hide and *squeak* again.

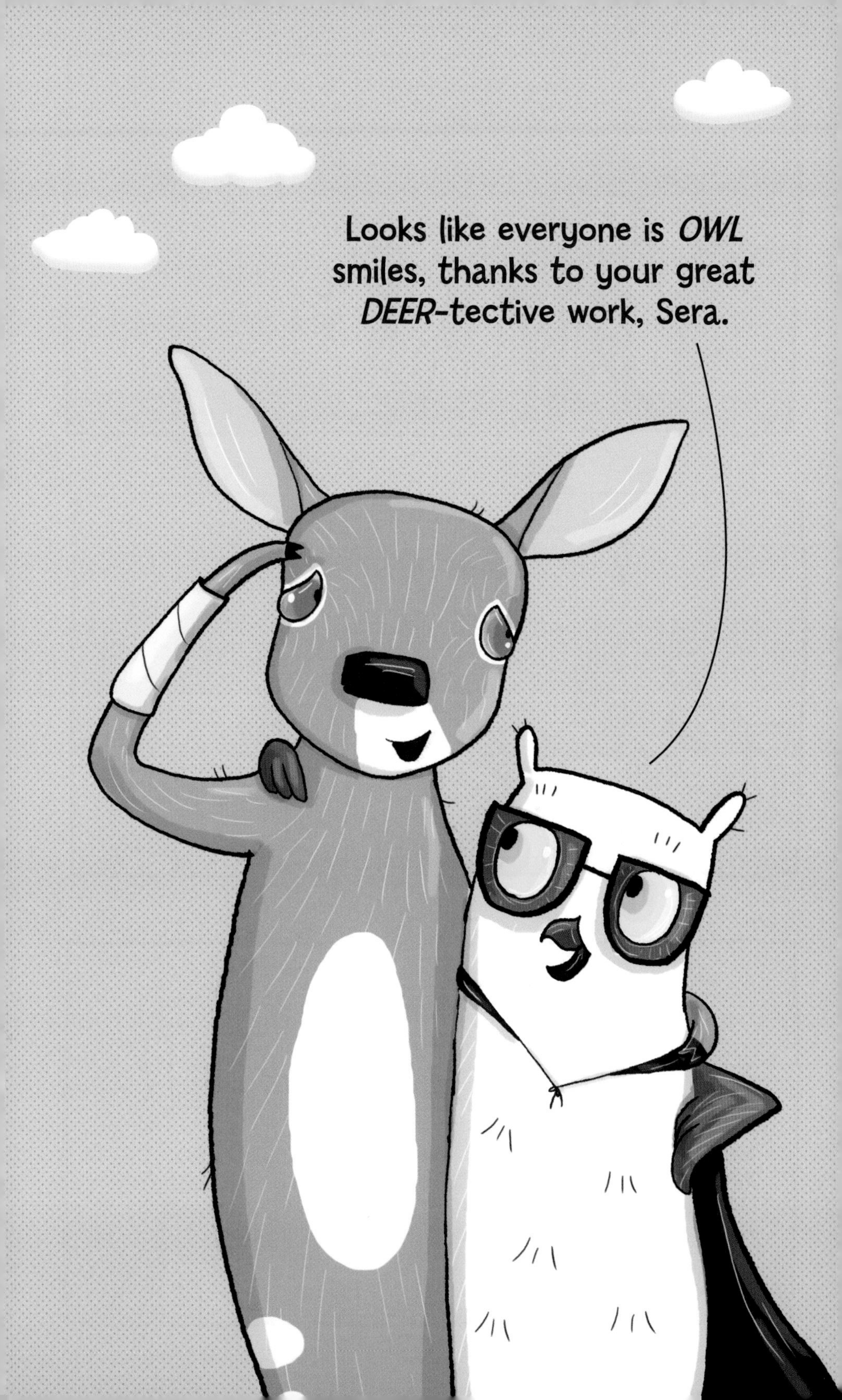
Looks like everyone is *OWL* smiles, thanks to your great *DEER*-tective work, Sera.

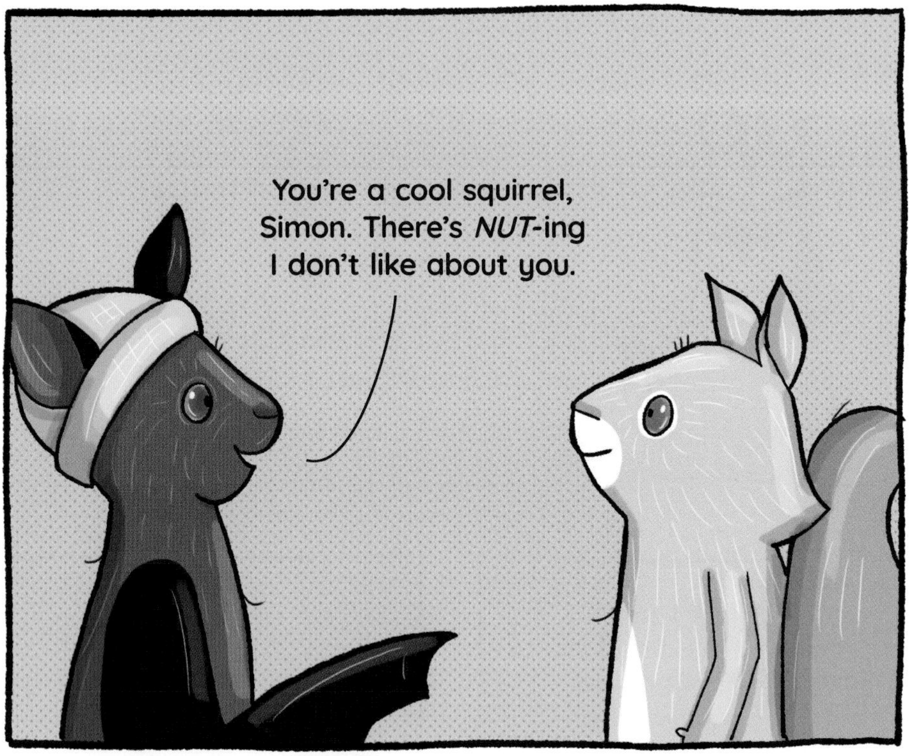
You're a cool squirrel, Simon. There's *NUT*-ing I don't like about you.

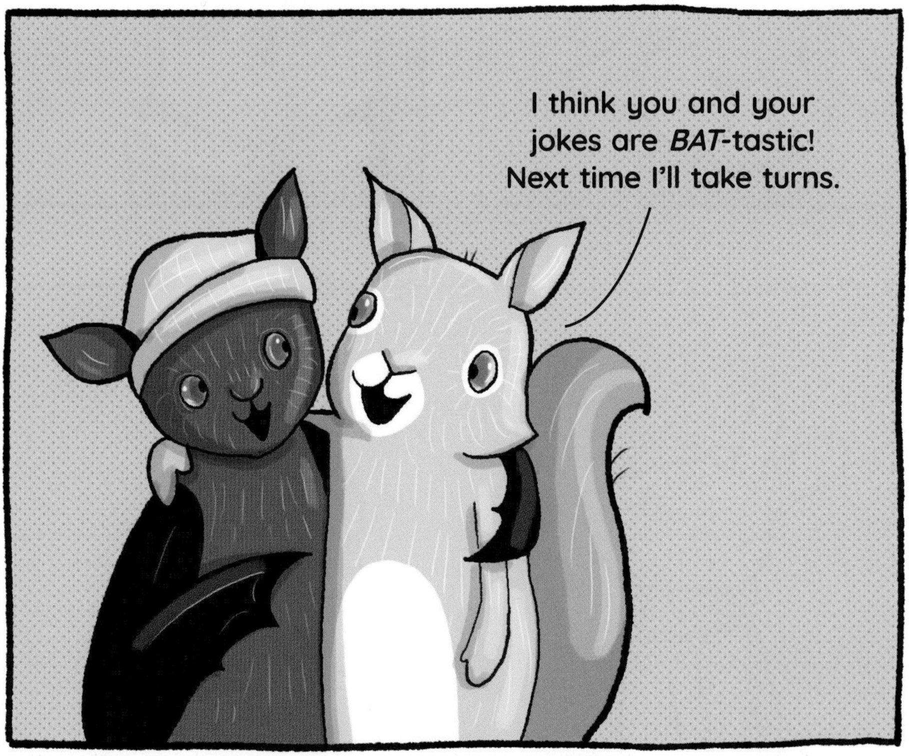
I think you and your jokes are *BAT*-tastic! Next time I'll take turns.

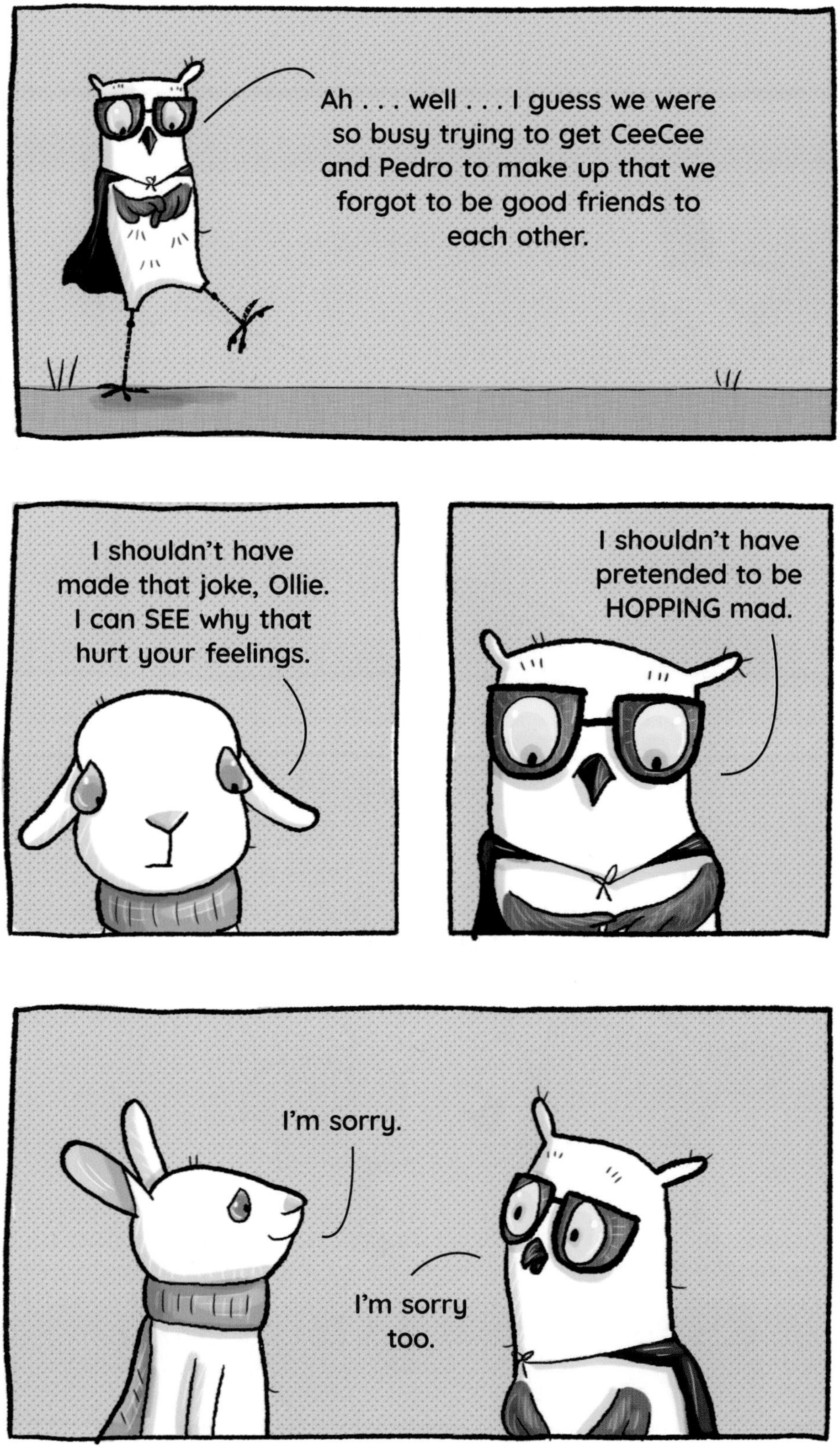
Ah . . . well . . . I guess we were so busy trying to get CeeCee and Pedro to make up that we forgot to be good friends to each other.
I shouldn't have made that joke, Ollie. I can SEE why that hurt your feelings.
I shouldn't have pretended to be HOPPING mad.
I'm sorry.
I'm sorry too.

Published by Picture Window Books, an imprint of Capstone
1710 Roe Crest Drive, North Mankato, Minnesota 56003
capstonepub.com

Text and illustrations copyright © 2023 by Renée Treml.

Library of Congress Cataloging-in-Publication Data is available
on the Library of Congress website.

ISBN: 9781666393866 (hardcover)
ISBN: 9781666396157 (paperback)
ISBN: 9781666396164 (ebook PDF)

Summary: When their friends get into an argument, Ollie and Bea step in to help.
Can they find a way to solve the *otter*-ly ridiculous kerfuffle?

Designed by Kay Fraser

Printed and bound in the USA. 5195

The Super Adventures of
OLLIE
AND
BEA
OTTER-LY RIDICULOUS

Here's Ollie and his best friend—

SHHH...

RENÉE TREML

PICTURE WINDOW BOOKS
a capstone imprint